LISTENING – HÖRVERSTÄNDNISÜBUNGEN

LÖSUNGEN UND NIEDERSCHRIFTEN (*TRANSCRIPTS*) ALLER HÖRTEXTE

A Hörverständnisübungen richtig üben

Meistens beginnt eine Schularbeit mit einer sogenannten Hörverständnisübung. Dabei wird ein Gespräch (oder ein Interview) auf Englisch zweimal abgespielt. Es ist wichtig, dass du genau hinhörst, damit du die Fragen richtig beantworten kannst.

Tipps und Tricks fürs Lösen von Hörverständnisübungen

Mache dich zuerst mit der Übung vertraut! Lies die Angabe genau durch, damit du weißt, was von dir verlangt wird. Es ist wichtig, dass dir bewusst ist, worauf du beim Hören achten sollst.
Ein hilfreicher Tipp ist, dass du dich beim ersten Mal Anhören nur mit dem Gespräch vertraut machst und ein Gefühl für die Hörverständnisübung bekommst. Vielen fällt es danach leichter, beim zweiten Durchgang die geforderten Aufgaben zu erfüllen.

Es gibt **verschiedene Arten von Übungen**, auf jede kannst du dich gut vorbereiten und einstellen.

- **Bei True / False-Aufgaben** musst du die angegebenen Sätze durchlesen und überprüfen, ob sie richtig (*true*) oder falsch (*false*) sind. Achte darauf, dass es sich im Normalfall um Kleinigkeiten handelt, die anders sind.

Zum Beispiel steht beim angegebenen Satz im Beispielkasten: Maxi geht **zweimal** die Woche zum Training, aber im Interview sagt er, dass er **viermal** wöchentlich Training hat, somit ist der Satz falsch und du musst False ankreuzen:

	True	False
Max plays football two times a week.	☐	☒

Es ist ganz wichtig, **immer eines der beiden Kästchen** anzukreuzen! Selbst, wenn du dir nach dem zweimaligen Hören noch nicht ganz sicher bist, kreuze das Kästchen an, das dir richtiger erscheint.

- Wenn du **zwischen mehreren Wörtern das richtige auswählen** musst, brauchst du wirklich nur auf das bestimmte Wort zu achten. Das macht diese Art der Überprüfung wahrscheinlich zur einfachsten Variante.

My schoolbag is *blue* / *green*.

Pass auf, dass du das richtige Wort wirklich eindeutig unterstreichst oder einkreist! Es muss für deine Lehrerin / deinen Lehrer nachvollziehbar sein, wofür du dich entschieden hast. Solltest du deine Meinung ändern und doch das andere Wort als richtig kennzeichnen, streiche das von dir falsch gewählte Wort ganz durch und kreise das richtige Wort wieder eindeutig ein.

- Häufig kommt es auch vor, dass du **in einer Lücke ein fehlendes Wort einsetzen** musst. Dabei ist es wichtig, dass du wirklich konzentriert und bewusst auf dieses Wort hinhörst, damit du es nicht versäumst. Oftmals kannst du im Verlauf des weiteren Gesprächs nachschauen, ob diese Phrase auch an einer anderen Stelle vorkommt. Eventuell steht hier das fehlende Wort und wird dir dann aus dem Zusammenhang klar. Wenn sich zum Beispiel die Sprecherinnen/die Sprecher während eines Gespräches/Interviews begrüßen oder verabschieden, sind diese Phrasen in der Regel gleich oder einander sehr ähnlich.

A: Goodbye, thank you!
B: ________________!
(Mit großer Wahrscheinlichkeit gehört auch hier *"Goodbye!"* oder *"Thank you!"* eingesetzt.)

Lösung:
A: Goodbye, thank you!
B: **Goodbye!**

- Manchmal musst du Sätze vervollständigen. Lies dir die Satzanfänge genau durch, um gut auf die fehlende Information achten zu können. Wenn du den Satz mit den Wörtern ergänzt, die du gehört hast, sollte es einen grammatikalisch richtigen, vollständigen Satz ergeben. Daher ist es besonders wichtig, dir im Anschluss den ganzen Satz noch einmal durchzulesen, um sicherzugehen, dass er Sinn ergibt.

Julie likes her ______________________.

Lösung:
Julie likes her **dog Rio very much**.

Jede Übung hilft dir dabei, sicherer zu werden und dich mit den verschiedenen Einsetzmöglichkeiten vertraut zu machen. Vergiss nicht, du wirst jedes Mal die Chance haben, die Hörverständnisübung zweimal in Folge zu hören!

Viel Spaß beim Zuhören!

Listening – Hörverständnisübungen

Alphabet

1 Listen and underline the letters of the alphabet you hear.

✱

A B C D E F G H I J K L M N O P Q R S T U V W X Y Z

Supergirl Lea

2 Listen to Lea introducing herself *(sich vorstellen)* and choose *am / is / are*.

✱

Hi, my name *is / are* Lea.

I *are / am* from Austria.

I *is / am* ten years old.

I *am / are* at school in Gmunden.

I *am / is* in class 1A.

My telephone number *are / is* 0555 – 4213769.

My email address *am / is* lea.supergirl@yeah.com

I *am / are* a super girl!

June's email

3 Listen to a dialogue about June's email address and fill in the missing words.

✱✱

Lena: Hi, I'm Lena. What's your ________________?

June: ________________, I'm June.

Lena: Hi, June. What's your ________________ address?

June: It's juneeliza@thatisme.com

Lena: ________________ you spell it for me?

June: Okay … j-u-n-e-e-l-i-z-a-at-t-h-a-t-i-s-m-e-dot-com.

Lena: ________________ you, June.

June: Goodbye, Lena.

Lena: ________________!

Numbers

4 Listen and write down the numbers.

____
____
____
____
____
____
____
____
____

Numbers and animals

5 Listen and fill in the numbers.

1 ______________ insects
2 ______________ gorillas
3 ______________ bears
4 ______________ crocodiles
5 ______________ frogs
6 ______________ fish
7 ______________ rabbits
8 ______________ cows

Frog meets bear

6 Listen to the dialogue and choose the missing *(fehlende)* words.

Frog: Hi. ________________ are you?

Bear: I'm ________________ thanks. How are you?

Frog: I'm okay. What's your ________________?

Bear: My name is Jake. I'm a brown ________________. And you?

Frog: I'm a green ________________. I'm Jenny. I eat flies.

Bear: Well, ________________ to meet you, Jenny. Bye!

Frog: ________________, Jake!

Boy meets girl

7 Listen to the dialogue and fill in the missing words.

Girl: Hi, Daniel. How are ________________?

Boy: Hi, Susie. I'm fine. ________________ are you?

Girl: I'm great. ________________ I have to go now. Goodbye!

Boy: ________________, Susie!

Children meet

8 Listen to the children and fill in the missing words.

Boy: Hi, Julie. How ________________ doing?

Girl 1: I'm fine, ________________ you. How are you, Samuel?

Boy: I'm fine. Julie, ________________ Melanie.

Girl 1: ________________, Melanie.

Girl 2: Hi, Julie.

Girl 1: Nice to ________________.

Girl 2: You ________________.

Girl 1: Goodbye!

Girl 2: ________________!

Boy: Goodbye, Julie!

Strange plural forms

9 Listen and fill in the missing numbers and irregular *(unregelmäßige)* plural forms.

1 five ____________________

2 ____________________

3 seven ____________________

4 ____________________

5 ten ____________________

6 ____________________

7 fifteen ____________________

8 ____________________

Alex

10 Listen to Alex introducing himself *(sich vorstellen)* and fill in the missing words.

1 Hi, ____________________ Alex.

2 I'm ____________________ years old.

3 ____________________ from Austria.

4 I'm in class ____________________.

5 My email address ____________________ alexisgreat@hello.com.

Jim's schoolbag

11 Listen and underline the things in Jim's schoolbag.

pen

pencil

pencil case

pencil sharpener

paintbrush

ruler

rubber

glue stick

scissors

water colours

Colours of classroom things

12 Listen and underline the correct colours of the classroom things.

1 glue stick – *blue / green*

2 exercise book – *yellow / orange*

3 pencil case – *pink / purple*

4 paintbrush – *red / black*

5 pencil sharpener – *white / grey*

6 ruler – *brown / green*

7 scissors – *grey / blue*

School things

13 Listen to Greg and Gina talking about their school things and fill in the correct colours.

1 Gina's new school bag is ____________________.

2 Greg's schoolbag is ____________________.

3 Greg's pencil case is ____________________.

4 Gina's pencil case is ____________________.

5 Gina's scissors are ____________________.

6 Gina's pencil sharpener is ____________________.

7 Greg's pencil sharpener is ____________________.

8 Greg's scissors are ____________________.

9 Greg's ruler is ____________________.

10 Greg's pen is ____________________.

11 Gina's ruler is ____________________.

12 Gina's pen is ____________________.

Colours in the classroom

14 ✱

Listen to Noah talking about the different colours of the things in his classroom and tick true or false.

	True	False
1 The door is blue.	☐	☐
2 The windows are white.	☐	☐
3 The board is green.	☐	☐
4 The desks are black.	☐	☐
5 The computer is grey.	☐	☐
6 The chairs are blue.	☐	☐
7 The floor is orange.	☐	☐
8 The CD player is pink.	☐	☐
9 The classroom is colourful.	☐	☐

Classroom imperatives

15 ✱✱

Listen to the teacher and write down the numbers in the correct order *(Reihenfolge)* of the imperatives *(Befehlsformen)*.

☐ Take out your books!

☐ Close the door!

☐ Don't speak!

☐ Clean the board!

☐ Stand up!

☐ Don't open the window!

☐ Open your books!

☐ Sit down!

Teacher's commands

16 ✱✱

Listen to what the teacher tells the students to do and complete *(vervollständige)* the commands *(Befehle)*.

1 ________________ your books!

2 ________________ down!

3 ________________ talk!

4 ________________ up!

5 ________________ the board!

6 ________________ the window!

7 ________________ your books!

8 ________________ the door!

9 ________________ the window!

10 ________________ up!

11 ________________ down!

In a terrarium

17 ✱✱✱

Listen to a dialogue of children looking into a terrarium and answer the questions about where the animals are.

1 Where is the snake?

____

2 Where is the crab?

____

3 Where are the spiders?

____

4 What are the spiders behind?

____

5 Where are the spiders NOT?

Üben

Tigers

18 ✱

Listen to Sara and Claire talking about tigers at the zoo and answer the questions.

	True	False
1 The tiger is next to the bush.	☐	☐
2 The tiger is not very beautiful.	☐	☐
3 Sara likes tigers.	☐	☐
4 Claire likes tigers.	☐	☐
5 Tigers are big.	☐	☐

Miguel's little sister Lilly

19 ✱

Listen to Miguel talking about his sister and choose *am / is / are*.

Hi, I *am / is* Miguel.

I *are / am* six years old.

I have a sister.

She *am / is* Lilly.

She *is / are* four years old.

She *am / is* nice to me.

I *am / is* nice to her.

We *is / are* a family.

Julie's family

20 ✱ Listen to Julie talking about her family and fill in *am / is / are*.

1 Hi, my name ________________ Julie.
2 I ________________ 35 years old.
3 I ________________ from America.
4 Daniel ________________ my husband *(Ehemann)*.
5 He ________________ also my best friend.
6 We ________________ married *(verheiratet)*.
7 We also ________________ parents.
8 Samuel and Melanie ________________ our children.
9 Samuel ________________ our son.
10 He ________________ six years old.
11 Melanie ________________ our daughter.
12 She ________________ three years old.
13 We ________________ a family.

David's desk

21 ✱✱ Listen to the description *(Beschreibung)* of David's desk and put the sentences into the correct order *(Reihenfolge)*.

☐ I love my cool desk!
☐ My grey CD-player is behind the pencil case.
☐ On my desk there is a black laptop with a blue pencil case next to it.
☐ In front of my pencil case there is my yellow exercise book.
☐ In the pencil case there are green pencils and a pencil sharpener.
☐ I have a wonderful new desk and all my school things are on it.
☐ My orange ruler is under the exercise book.

Üben

Pirate Paula

22 ✱✱

Listen to Pirate Paula introducing herself *(sich vorstellen)* and tick *(kreuze an)* true or false.

		True	False
1	Paula is a pirate.	☐	☐
2	She has got a pelican on her shoulder.	☐	☐
3	She has got a dog next to her.	☐	☐
4	Paula has got a wooden leg.	☐	☐
5	Paula has not got a sword.	☐	☐
6	The pirate has got pink hair.	☐	☐
7	Paula, the pirate, hasn't got a big ship.	☐	☐
8	She hasn't got a fast ship.	☐	☐
9	The pirate has got a tattoo on her arm.	☐	☐
10	Paula has got purple shoes.	☐	☐

Pirate Kate

23 ✱✱

Listen to Pirate Kate introducing herself *(sich vorstellen)* and tick *(kreuze an)* true or false.

		True	False
1	Captain Kate has got blond hair and blue eyes.	☐	☐
2	Pirate Kate has got a tattoo of a parrot on her arm.	☐	☐
3	Kate has not got a wooden leg.	☐	☐
4	She has got a black and white dog.	☐	☐
5	Pirate Kate has got a big nose with a ring in it.	☐	☐
6	She is very strong!	☐	☐
7	Her father 'James the Joker' is also a pirate.	☐	☐
8	James is not very funny.	☐	☐
9	He has got a small nose and red hair.	☐	☐
10	James has got a hook and a wooden leg.	☐	☐
11	Pirate James has got a parrot.	☐	☐

Feelings in the classroom

24 ✱✱

Listen to Tom describing the feelings of the children in the classroom and fill in the correct feelings.

1 Tom is ____________________

2 Lisa is ____________________

3 Ben is ____________________

4 Lea is ____________________

5 Aaron is ____________________

6 Debbie is ____________________

7 Vicky is ____________________

8 Tina is ____________________

9 Tom is ____________________

10 Ann is ____________________

Supermodel Jane

25 ✱

Listen to the description *(Beschreibung)* of a day in the life of Supermodel Jane and underline *(unterstreiche)* the correct feelings.

Jane is a supermodel. This is a day in the life of Supermodel Jane.

It is early in the morning and Jane is *excited / tired*. She has got a beautiful body and a great job. Jane is *proud / happy*.

At work there are many photographers. They have got cameras.

They are *nervous / excited*. Jane is *happy / excited*. She has a good job.

She is not *bored / nervous*.

At lunchtime Jane is *angry / hungry*. She has not got a hamburger, she has got an apple. So Jane is *hungry / angry*.

In the afternoon it is *cold / hot*. So Jane is very hot, she is not *sad / cold*.

In the evening Jane is not at work. She is at home. She is *scared / bored*.

At night Jane is in bed. She is *tired / sad*.

Barbara's week

26 Listen to Barbara talking about her week and connect *(verbinde)* the sentences.

✱✱

On Monday	1
On Tuesday	2
On Wednesday	3
On Thursday	4
On Friday	5
On Saturday	6
On Sunday	7

A	I am happy, I have dance class. I love dancing.
B	I am nervous, I have a test. I am not proud.
C	I am excited, it is the weekend! I am not bored!
D	I am sad, I am not okay.
E	I am angry, I am not happy.
F	I am cold, very cold. I am not hot.
G	I am hungry. Oh! I am very hungry!

Our band

27 Listen to the band leader *(Leiter)* Miguel introducing *(vorstellen)* himself and his band and fill in the missing words.

✱✱

1 Miguel is the ______________________________.

2 Melissa is the ______________________________.

3 Martin is the ______________________________.

4 Marvin is the ______________________________.

5 Marcus is the ______________________________.

6 Marie is the ______________________________.

7 M's is the ______________________________.

Samuel's family

28 Listen to Samuel talking about his family and fill in *I, you, he, she, it, we* or *they*.

✱

Hi, I am Samuel. __________ am six years old.

__________ have a big house and my own room. I like __________.

My daddy is 36 years old. __________ works in Vienna. My mum is also 36 years old.

__________ is a teacher.

Interview with Samuel

29 Listen to the interview with Samuel and choose the correct form of *I, you, he, she* or *it*.

Girl: Hello, what's your name?

Boy: Hello, my name is Samuel.

Girl: How old are *you / they*?

Boy: *He / I* am six years old.

Girl: Where do you live?

Boy: *I / We* live in Austria.

Girl: What is your house like?

Boy: *It / He* is big.

Girl: Okay ... do *you / they* have a brother or a sister?

Boy: I have a sister.

Girl: What's her name?

Boy: Her name is Melanie.

Girl: How old is she?

Boy: *He / She* is four years old.

Girl: And what does your father do?

Boy: My father works in Vienna.

Girl: How old is *she / he*?

Boy: *He / She* is 36 years old.

Girl: And what does your mother do?

Boy: My mother goes to school.

Girl: Okay ... and how old is *it / she*?

Boy: *They / She* is 36 years old.

Girl: And what is her job at school?

Boy: *She / He* is a teacher.

Girl: Okay, thank you very much. Have a good day. Goodbye!

Boy: Goodbye, Julie!

Üben

What Beth and Maria can and can't do

30 ✱✱

Listen to Beth and Maria talking about what they can and can't do and fill in the missing words.

Beth: Hi Maria!

Maria: Hi Beth!

Beth: Maria, look what I ________________ do!

Maria: Wow Beth! You ________________ wiggle your ears! I ________________ do that. What else ________________ you do?

Beth: Well, I ________________ stand on my hands. Do you want to see? I ________________ show you.

Maria: Yes, please … wow, you ________________ really stand on your hands. I ________________ stand on my hands.

Beth: That's okay. What ________________ you do?

Maria: Well, I ________________ touch my nose with my tongue.

Beth: Really? ________________ you show me?

Maria: Yes, I ________________ see?

Beth: Oh, that is great! I ________________ touch my nose with my tongue.

Maria: Fine, but you ________________ try.

Beth: Okay … hm … yeah! I ________________ touch my nose with my tongue!

Maria: Oh, yes you ________________ do it!

Mike's school day

31 ✱✱

Listen to Mike talking about his school day and fill in the missing words in present simple *(einfache Gegenwart)*.

1 In the morning I ________________ at seven and get ready.

2 Then I ________________ to school.

3 There I ________________ my friends.

4 We often laugh and ________________ fun.

5 In English we ________________ to our partners.

6 In music we ________________ to CDs.

7 In German we ________________ a text.

8 Next we ________________ lunch.

9 In gym we ________________ very much.

10 That ________________ my school day.

Milo, the cat

32 ✱✱✱

Listen to Patricia talking about her cat and answer the questions.

		True	False
1	The cat Milo is four years old.	☐	☐
2	Milo likes to drink water.	☐	☐
3	The cat looks for dogs when she is outside.	☐	☐

4 Milo loves to …
A sleep on the couch **B** sit on the couch **C** play on the couch

5 The cat is …
A small and black **B** small and slow **C** small but fast

6 When Patricia comes home Milo …
A makes a lot of noise **B** runs away very fast **C** likes to eat her snack

7 Patricia carries ________________________________.

8 Milo sleeps ________________________________.

9 Milo is ________________________________.

What my family eats

33 ✱ Listen to a mother talking about what her family eats and answer the questions.

	True	False
Elizabeth's family likes to eat noodles.	☐	☐
They often eat rice.	☐	☐
Elizabeth eats lots of salad.	☐	☐
The children like vegetables.	☐	☐
Daniel always eats cheese.	☐	☐
He doesn't like fish.	☐	☐
The family usually has noodles with sausages.	☐	☐
The children always have an apple for breakfast.	☐	☐
They sometimes have ice-cream for snack.	☐	☐
The family often has pizza.	☐	☐

Dialogue about clothes

34 ✱✱ Listen to Mia and Marcy talking about clothes and choose the correct words.

Mia: Hi Marcy!

Marcy: Hey Mia!

Mia: Marcy, I love your ***skirt / sweater***. Is it new?

Marcy: Yes, it is. I ***often / don't often*** wear pink but I like this new pink sweater.

Mia: ***Does / Do*** you buy your own clothes?

Marcy: Yes, I do. And you? Do you buy your own ***clothes / shoes*** too?

Mia: No I ***don't / doesn't***.

Marcy: So, ***do / does*** your mum buy your clothes for you?

Mia: Yes, she does. She knows that I like to wear dresses and ***shirts / skirts***. I have a new dress!

Marcy: That's nice. What colour is your new ***blouse / dress***?

Mia: ***It's / They're*** blue and yellow and white.

Marcy: That ***dress / cap*** sounds nice!

Mia: Do you like to wear ***trousers / dresses***?

Marcy: No, I don't like to wear dresses or skirts. I often wear jeans and ***trainers / T-shirts***.

Lilly's dream pet

35 ✱✱

Listen to an interview about Lilly's dream pet and answer the questions.

Lilly: Hello!

Alara: Hi, tell me about your dream pet!

Lilly: Well, my dream pet is an unicorn.

Alara: ______________________________?

Lilly: It's a unicorn … that is my favourite pet.

Alara: Okay ______________________________?

Lilly: It's Mr. Perfect.

Alara: I understand ______________________________?

Lilly: Mr. Perfect lives in a stable in my garden. He has a lot of room.

Alara: Alright ______________________________?

Lilly: He eats lots of hay *(Heu)*, just like a horse, and also fruit.

Alara: Sure ______________________________?

Lilly: I feed my favourite pet five times a day.

Alara: Wow! That's really a lot!

Lilly: Yes, my unicorn is BIG!

Alara: One last question: ______________________________?

Lilly: No! My unicorn is a dream pet!

Problems with unusual pets

36 ✱✱

Listen to Taylor's problem with his unusual pet and fill in the missing object pronouns *me, you, him, her, it, us* or *them*.

Let me tell you about a problem I have with my unusual pet.

It is a crocodile and I love ________________!

I call him Mr. Long because he has a lot of very long teeth.

The problem is that I have to clean ________________!

It takes a very long time and I don't like to brush Mr. Long's teeth.

Can you understand ________________?

I really like my unusual pet and I know that Mr. Long likes ________________.

We can play in the swimming pool and he is nice to ________________.

I just have another problem: I can't pet *(streicheln)* ________________.

It hurts because he is not very soft and comfortable.

He's a crocodile and I can feel ________________.

One more problem is that Mr. Long likes to play outside. There he looks for bugs *(Käfer)* and mice and when he finds some, Mr. Long brings them to ________________.

It is strange because I don't like bugs and mice. I hate ________________!

Üben

Shopping dialogue

37 ✱✱✱

Listen to the shopping dialogue and put the sentences into the correct order *(Reihenfolge)*, the beginning and ending are given *(vorgegeben)*.

- [ ] *Shop assistant:* That's 9,95.
- [ ] *Shop assistant:* Okay… do you like that one over there?
- [ ] *Shop assistant:* Would you like this one here?
- [1] *Shop assistant:* Hello, can I help you?
- [ ] *Shop assistant:* What colour?
- [ ] *Shop assistant:* Let me see. How about this one here?
- [17] *Shop assistant:* You're welcome. Goodbye!
- [ ] *Shop assistant:* Would you like one of those caps over there?
- [ ] *Shop assistant:* Then what cap would you like?

- [ ] *Child:* How much is it?
- [2] *Child:* Hello. Yes, please. I want a new cap.
- [ ] *Child:* That's perfect. Thank you very much.
- [ ] *Child:* No, I think it's too big.
- [ ] *Child:* One of these right here, please.
- [ ] *Child:* No, they do not look cool.
- [ ] *Child:* Yes, I do. But it is too expensive.
- [18] *Child:* Goodbye!
- [ ] *Child:* I like black and red.

How much is / are

38 Listen to the shopping dialogue and fill in *how much is / are*.

Shop assistant: Hello, can I help you?
Tom: Hi, Yes please. ____________________ that sweater?
Shop assistant: That sweater is 19,50.
Tom: Okay, ____________________ those jeans?
Shop assistant: Those jeans are 25,90.
Tom: Alright, ____________________ this hat?
Shop assistant: This hat is 7,95.
Tom: And ____________________ shoes?
Shop assistant: Those shoes are 15,90.
Tom: Fine, thank you.
Shop assistant: What would you like?
Tom: I don't want anything, thanks.

Midnight in Vienna

39 Listen to the time differences *(Zeitunterschiede)* and write down the correct times.

1 When it's midnight in Vienna what's the time in New York?

____

2 When it's midnight in Vienna what's the time in London?

____

3 When it's midnight in Vienna what's the time in Sydney?

____

4 When it's midnight in Vienna what's the time in Tokyo?

____

5 When it's midnight in Vienna what's the time in Moscow?

____

6 When it's midnight in Vienna what's the time in Cairo?

____

A day in the life of Vicky

40 ✱✱✱

Listen to Vicky talking about a day in her life and answer the questions.

		True	False
1	Vicky gets up at half past six.	☐	☐
2	She has breakfast at seven.	☐	☐
3	School starts at a quarter past eight.	☐	☐

4 Vicky goes to ballet class at ______________________________.

5 Vicky plays with her friends from ______________________________.

6 She has dinner with her family at ______________________________.

7 From seven to eight Vicky …
A does her homework **B** talks on the phone **C** watches TV

8 At half past eight she …
A goes to bed **B** has a bath **C** goes home

9 Until nine o'clock Vicky …
A plays computer games **B** reads a book **C** listens to music

Phone conversation

41 ✱✱✱

Listen to a phone conversation *(Gespräch)* about what different people are doing at the moment and fill in present progressive.

1 Ben: ______________________________

2 Lea: ______________________________

3 Jeff: ______________________________

4 Jane: ______________________________

5 Lea's dad: ______________________________

6 Lea's mum: ______________________________

7 Ben: ______________________________

What are different people doing right now?

42 * * *

Listen to what the different people are doing at the moment and put the sentences into the correct order *(Reihenfolge)*, the beginning and ending are given *(vorgegeben)*.

☐	Amy is doing her homework.
☐	Barney is playing a game with his friend.
☐	Christine is reading a book.
☐	Danielle is texting her boyfriend on her phone.
☐	Eliza is writing a long text.
1	Francis is swimming in our pool.
15	Greg is skateboarding with his classmates.
☐	Hannah is looking after her three cats.
☐	Iris is having a snack.
☐	Jane is cooking dinner for her family.
☐	Karin is riding her bike to school.
☐	Lorenz is talking to his neighbour.
☐	Mike is listening to music on the couch.
☐	Nico is eating chocolate in bed.
☐	Pete is watching a funny film in the living room.

Birthday invitation

43 * *

Listen to Ann and Beth talking about a birthday invitation *(Einladung)* and tick true or false.

		True	False
1	Ann is going to have a birthday party.	☐	☐
2	Her birthday party is going to be on the seventh.	☐	☐
3	Beth is not going to come to Ann's birthday party.	☐	☐
4	They are going to eat cake and play games.	☐	☐
5	Ann's mum is not going to bake the cake.	☐	☐
6	They are going to have a garden party at Ann's house.	☐	☐
7	Ann is going to invite seven friends to her party.	☐	☐
8	Beth is going to buy Ann a birthday present.	☐	☐

Tina's and Tom's date

44 ✱✱

Listen to Tina and Tom talking about when they can go to the cinema and fill in the correct dates.

1 Tina has a tennis match on the ____________________.

2 Tina has a friend's birthday party on the ____________________.

3 Tom has a football game on the ____________________.

4 Tom has a big family dinner party on the ____________________.

5 Tina has a test on the ____________________.

6 Tina has to study on the ____________________.

7 Tom has a concert on the ____________________.

8 Tina has a ski trip from the sixteenth until the ____________________.

9 Tina and Tom can go to the cinema ____________________.

Arielle's birthday plans

45 ✱✱✱

Listen to Arielle talking about her birthday plans and put the sentences into the correct order *(Reihenfolge)*.

☐ I am going to have a party at my house.

☐ At night we are going to talk and eat sweets.

☐ I am going to get a lot of presents and play with them.

☐ First we are going to play games in the house and also in the garden.

☐ Then we are going to eat chips and drink Cola.

☐ Later we are going to make a disco and dance to cool music.

☐ My birthday is on the nineteenth and it is a Friday this year.

☐ It's going to be the best birthday in my life!

☐ My mum is going to make a pink birthday cake because that is my favourite colour.

☐ Then my friends are all going to sleep at my house.

☐ I am going to invite my three best friends and we are going to have lots of fun.

☐ In the evening we are going to watch funny films and eat popcorn.

☐ In the morning we are going to be tired and we are not going to get up early.

Last night

46 ✱ ✱

Listen to John and Lisa talking about where they were last night and underline *(unterstreiche)* the correct forms.

John: Hi Lisa! Were you ***in bed / at home*** last night? I came to your house but your family was not there.

Lisa: Hey John! Really? When were you at my ***house / hall*** last night?

John: I was at your house at half past seven.

Lisa: At half past seven I was in the ***bath / bed*** because I was ***hot / cold***. I was at home.

John: Were your parents at home?

Lisa: Yes, my parents were at home. They were in the ***living room / kitchen***. They were ***happy / hungry***.

John: Okay, was your brother at home?

Lisa: My brother was in the ***living room / bedroom***. The TV was on. He was ***scared / sad***.

John: Was your sister at home?

Lisa: No, she was not at home. Sue was in the ***library (Bibliothek) / park*** with her boyfriend.

She was ***happy / hungry***. They were ***alone / angry***. When were you at home?

John: I was at my house at eight p.m. I was in my ***bedroom / bathroom***. I was ***scared / angry***.

Lisa: I am ***sad / angry*** you were not with us.

Last weekend

47 * * *

Listen to Benny talking about his last weekend and answer the questions.

		True	False
1	Last weekend wasn't great for Benny.	☐	☐
2	Benny was at the cinema with a friend.	☐	☐
3	The film wasn't good.	☐	☐
4	The boys were at a Chinese restaurant for dinner.	☐	☐

5 The boys *were / weren't* at a bowling centre.

6 In the evening Benny *wasn't / was* tired.

7 In the morning he *wasn't / was* tired.

8 After breakfast Benny *wasn't / was* at his friend's house.

9 For lunch the boys were at a pizza place but the food ______________________.

10 In the afternoon they were at a shopping centre for ______________________.

11 In the evening Benny was at home, he was ______________________.

12 For Benny the weekend was ______________________.

Yesterday

48 * *

Yesterday at seven o'clock Jonathan was on the phone with Susan. There was a lot going on at her house. Listen to her story and tick true or false.

		True	False
1	Yesterday at seven o'clock the family wasn't busy.	☐	☐
2	Susan's brother was in his room at his desk.	☐	☐
3	He wasn't angry.	☐	☐
4	Susan wasn't in the bathtub.	☐	☐
5	Susan's sister was warm and relaxed.	☐	☐
6	Susan was on the couch.	☐	☐
7	She was bored.	☐	☐
8	Susan's dad was at home.	☐	☐
9	He was not happy.	☐	☐
10	He was angry.	☐	☐
11	Susan's mum was in the kitchen.	☐	☐
12	She was hungry.	☐	☐
13	Yesterday at seven Jonathan wasn't at home.	☐	☐

Ambulance / Fire Brigade / Police

49 ✱✱✱ Listen to the different phone conversations and fill in the missing information.

Dialogue 1

Rescue: Ambulance, fire brigade or police?

Child: ______________________, please.

…

Ambulance: Hello, ______________________?

Child: I need to go to the ______________________! I jumped in the trampoline and now there is blood on my head!

Ambulance: What's the ______________________?

Child: I live in ______________________ 23.

Ambulance: Can you ______________________, please?

Child: Yes, It's ______________________.

Ambulance: ______________________ on our way.

Dialogue 2

Rescue: Ambulance, fire brigade or ______________________?

Child: Police, ______________________.

…

Police: ______________________, how can I help?

Child: There was a robbery ______________________!

Police: Okay, ______________________?

Child: I am on ______________________.

Police: ______________________ for me, please?

Child: Yes, It's ______________________.

Police: ______________________, we are on our way.

Dialogue 3

Rescue: ______________________________, fire brigade or police?

Child: ______________________________, please.

…

Fire Brigade: How can ______________________________?

Child: ______________________________ in my kitchen!

Fire Brigade: Oh, ______________________________?

Child: I live in ______________________________.

Fire Brigade: Uhm … Can you ______________________________?

Child: It's ______________________________.

Fire Brigade: Okay, we are ______________________________.

Rescue from a fire

50 Listen to a story about a fire and put the sentences into the correct order *(Reihenfolge)*.

- [ ] There was a fire!
- [ ] The family watched the fire brigade stop the fire.
- [ ] When she arrived back in the kitchen she jumped!
- [ ] The children were in the bathtub, they were warm.
- [ ] She shouted 'Help!' and spelled the address of her house.
- [ ] They rescued the children from the bathtub.
- [ ] On Wednesday 17th there was a fire in a kitchen.
- [ ] The children called their mum and she walked upstairs to the bathroom.
- [ ] The children played in the water and they were happy.
- [ ] In the end the family was happy and safe, but sad that the kitchen was broken.
- [ ] The children were cold and scared.
- [ ] Suddenly the mother smelled smoke.
- [ ] She tried to stop it but the fire was too big, so she phoned the fire brigade.
- [ ] The mother cooked dinner because the family was hungry.
- [ ] Next she waited for five minutes and then the fire brigade arrived.

Manuel's afternoon

51 ✱✱

Listen to Manuel talking about his afternoon and fill in the missing verbs in past simple *(Mitvergangenheitsform)*.

Yesterday ________________ a very sunny day.

After school I ________________ home.

I was happy because my mother ________________ lasagne for lunch.

Later I ________________ my friend Niklas in the afternoon.

Next I ________________ for fifteen minutes and then Niklas ________________.

We ________________ football outside and then it ________________.

Niklas ________________ and ________________ me.

I was hurt and so I ________________ at him.

He ________________ me up and ________________ me back inside the house.

After that I ________________ to rest and so we ________________ TV on the couch.

Finally Niklas ________________ goodbye and ________________ back home.

TV habits

52 ✱✱

Listen to Claudia and Patrick talking about their TV habits *(Gewohnheiten)* and tick true or false.

Claudia:	True	False
Claudia usually watches TV for about three hours every day.	☐	☐
Claudia likes to watch cartoons when she eats breakfast.	☐	☐
She watches science fiction shows before she goes to bed.	☐	☐
Her parents usually watch the news at eight o'clock.	☐	☐
Her brother sometimes watches sports programmes.	☐	☐

Patrick:	True	False
Patrick usually watches TV for about two hours on the weekend.	☐	☐
He sometimes watches sports programmes after lunch.	☐	☐
On the weekend Patrick watches movies with his family.	☐	☐
His little sister likes films about animals.	☐	☐
Patrick likes to watch films about superheroes.	☐	☐

Past Tense

53 ✱✱

Listen and write down the irregular past tense forms.

1 ______________________

2 ______________________

3 ______________________

4 ______________________

5 ______________________

6 ______________________

7 ______________________

8 ______________________

9 ______________________

10 ______________________

11 ______________________

12 ______________________

13 ______________________

14 ______________________

15 ______________________

16 ______________________

17 ______________________

18 ______________________

19 ______________________

20 ______________________

Barbara's bad dream

54 ✱

Listen to a Barbara talking about her bad dream and choose the correct past forms *(Mitvergangenheit)*.

Last night I *read / saw* a scary book and then I *took / went* to bed.

I *had / was* a bad dream and I *took / woke* up in the night.

I *held / thought* it was real and I *met / was* scared.

Next I *put / heard* a strange noise and *sat / rang* up in bed.

Then I *said / saw* a light on and *paid / froze*.

Suddenly I *took / ran* into my parents' room and I *had / held* my mum's hand.

Young love

55 ✱✱✱

Listen to a story about young love and answer the questions.

		True	False
1	When the man was young he met a girl.	☐	☐
2	He saw her after school and phoned her.	☐	☐
3	They went to the park and sat on a bench.	☐	☐

4 There they held hands and ______________________________.

5 They had a good time because ______________________________.

6 The young man put his arm around her and ______________________________.

7 They took a walk and …
A sang a love song **B** ran in the grass **C** saw a beautiful bird

8 But the young man froze because …
A the girl was gone **B** the girl was so lovely **C** the girl said: 'I love you!'

9 When he heard her say it, suddenly …
A the man ran away **B** the man was shocked **C** the man read a book

Princess Grace

56 ✱✱

Listen to a story about Princess Grace and fill in the missing words.

Hello, my ______________ is Grace.

I want to tell you about my ______________.

When I was a little ______________ I watched a movie with a very beautiful actress.

That was when I decided that I also wanted to ______________ an actress.

I went to ______________ and studied very hard and after a while my dream came true.

I ______________ an actress!

I played in many movies and I soon became a ______________.

One day I met a very ______________ young man and we got along very well.

We went out and we had a lot of fun and soon we fell in ______________.

He told ______________ that he was a prince and I was so surprised and shocked!

I couldn't believe ______________!

Soon he asked me to be ______________ wife and I said: 'YES!'

We ______________ married.

I love my prince so ______________ and now I am Princess Grace.

Somedays my life seems ______________ a dream.

Arruba's story

57 ✱✱

Listen to Arruba's story and answer the questions.

		True	False
1	Arruba is called the king of the desert.	☐	☐
2	She thinks her name is interesting.	☐	☐
3	She didn't travel a lot when she was young.	☐	☐
4	Arruba's dad travelled for work.	☐	☐
5	She liked eating desserts.	☐	☐
6	Arruba likes riding bikes.	☐	☐
7	She likes the quiet desert.	☐	☐
8	People asked Arruba questions about the desert.	☐	☐
9	They wanted to learn about the desert.	☐	☐
10	Arruba is not called the queen of the desert.	☐	☐

B Hörübungen für die erste Schularbeit

Mia is great

58 ✱

Listen to Mia introducing herself *(sich vorstellen)* and choose *am/is/are.*

Hello, how *is / are* you?

My name *is / are* Mia.

I *are / am* from England.

I *is / am* 15 years old.

I *am / are* at school in London.

I *am / is* in class 5B.

My telephone number *are / is* 0678 – 9753246.

My email address *am / is* miaisgreat@home.com

I *am / are* a great girl!

And how *is / are* you?

Numbers

59 ✱

Listen to the numbers and write them down.

____

____

____

____

____

____

____

____

____

Mouse meets elephant

60 Listen to the dialogue and fill in the missing *(fehlende)* words.

Mouse: Hi. ________________ are you?

Elephant: Hi, I'm ________________ thanks. How are you?

Mouse: I'm okay. What's your ________________?

Elephant: My name is Eliot. I'm a grey elephant. And ________________?

Mouse: ________________ a brown mouse. I'm Minnie. I eat cheese.

Elephant: ________________ to meet you, Minnie. I eat mice!

Mouse: Oh no! ________________!

Dialogue

61 Listen to the dialogue and fill in the missing *(fehlende)* words.

Jules: Hi, Dee. ________________ are you?

Dee: Hi, Jules. I'm fine, thanks. How ________________ you?

Jules: ________________ great. How is your brother?

Dee: He is okay, ________________ I have to go now.

Jules: Have a nice day! ________________!

Dee: Bye!

Strange plural forms

62 Listen and fill in the numbers and irregular *(unregelmäßige)* plural forms.

1 fifteen ________________

2 ________________

3 two ________________

4 ________________

5 three ________________

6 ________________

7 twenty-one ________________

8 ________________

Colours of classroom things

63 ✱

Listen and underline the correct colours of the classroom things.

pencil case – *pink / purple*

paintbrush – *blue / black*

pencil sharpener – *white / yellow*

ruler – *blue / black*

glue stick – *green / grey*

exercise book – *orange / yellow*

scissors – *grey / green*

book – *brown / red*

Colours in the classroom

64 ✱✱

Listen to Norah talking about the different colours of the things in her classroom and tick true or false.

		True	False
1	The door is blue.	☐	☐
2	The windows are black.	☐	☐
3	The board is green.	☐	☐
4	The desks are black.	☐	☐
5	The computer is white.	☐	☐
6	The chairs are blue.	☐	☐
7	The floor is orange.	☐	☐
8	The CD player is purple.	☐	☐

Teacher's commands

65 ✱✱✱

Listen to what the teacher tells the students to do and complete *(vervollständige)* the commands *(Befehle)*.

1 ____________________ up!

2 ____________________ the door!

3 ____________________ down!

4 ____________________ your books!

5 ____________________ the window!

6 ____________________ the board!

7 ____________________ up!

8 ____________________ talk!

C Hörübungen für die zweite Schularbeit

Giraffes

66 ✱

Listen to Sara and Claire talking about giraffes at the zoo and answer the questions.

	True	False
1 The giraffe is next to the tree.	☐	☐
2 The giraffe is not beautiful.	☐	☐
3 Sara likes giraffes.	☐	☐
4 Claire likes giraffes.	☐	☐
5 Giraffes are big.	☐	☐

Deena's family

67 ✱

Listen to Deena talking about her family and fill in *am / is / are*.

1 Hi, my name ________________ Deena.

2 I ________________ 26 years old.

3 I ________________ from England.

4 It ________________ lovely there.

5 My brother's name ________________ Henry.

6 He ________________ my baby brother.

7 My sister's name ________________ Nina.

8 She ________________ my big sister.

9 We ________________ a family.

Üben

Princess Pia

68 ✱✱

Listen to Princess Pia introducing herself *(sich vorstellen)* and tick *(kreuze an)* true or false.

	True	False
1 Pia is a princess.	☐	☐
2 She has got a pelican on her shoulder.	☐	☐
3 She has got a dog next to her.	☐	☐
4 Pia hasn't got a tattoo.	☐	☐
5 Pia has got a sword.	☐	☐
6 The princess has got purple hair.	☐	☐
7 Pia, the princess has got a nose stud.	☐	☐
8 She hasn't got a big castle.	☐	☐

Belinda's week

69 ✱✱

Listen to Belinda talking about her week and connect *(verbinde)* the sentences.

On Monday	1
On Tuesday	2
On Wednesday	3
On Thursday	4
On Friday	5
On Saturday	6
On Sunday	7

A	I am nervous, I have music class.
B	I am hungry, very hungry. I am angry!
C	I am hot, I am not cold.
D	I am happy, I love the weekend!
E	I am excited. Oh! I am very excited!
F	I am sad, I have a test.
G	I am tired, I am not okay.

Denise's family

70 ✱✱

Listen to Denise talking about her family and fill in *I, you, he, she, it, we* or *they*.

Hi, my name is Denise. ______________ am sixteen years old.

______________ have a big brother.

______________ is 18 years old.

______________ is a student at university.

And my sister is 20. ______________ is a manager.

My parents are from India. ______________ live in a nice house.

______________ is very big.

______________ are a happy family.

Do ______________ have a big family?

Marvin, the dog

71 ✱✱✱

Listen to Penny talking about her dog and answer the questions.

		True	False
1	The dog Marvin is four years old.	☐	☐
2	Marvin likes to watch TV.	☐	☐
3	The dog looks for balls when it is outside.	☐	☐

4 Marvin loves to …
A sleep on the couch **B** sit on the couch **C** play on the couch

5 The dog plays with …
A dogs and toys **B** dogs and balls **C** dolls and toys

6 Marvin is …
A a big dog **B** a small dog **C** a big cat

7 Marvin cannot ____.

8 Marvin is ____.

9 Penny loves ____.

D Hörübungen für die dritte Schularbeit

Dialogue about clothes

72 ✱

Listen to Rebecca and Angela talking about clothes and choose the correct words.

Rebecca: Hi Angela!
Angela: Hey Rebecca!
Rebecca: Wow, Angela I love your *skirt / shirt* … is it new?
Angela: Yes, thanks … it is. I *always / often* wear blue. I like this colour.
Rebecca: *Does / Do* you often buy clothes?
Angela: Yes, I do … And you? Do you also like to buy *clothes / sweets*?
Rebecca: No, I *don't / do*.
Angela: Really?
Rebecca: My *mother / sister* gives me her clothes.
Angela: That's nice. Is that skirt *old / new*?
Rebecca: Yes, it is.
Angela: Well it's *nice / okay*!
Rebecca: Do you like to wear *T-shirts / skirts*?
Angela: No, I don't like to wear skirts. I often wear jeans and *shoes / T-shirts*.

Shopping dialogue

73 ✱✱

Listen to a shopping dialogue and put the sentences into the correct order *(Reihenfolge)*, the beginning and ending are given *(vorgegeben)*.

☐	*Shop assistant:*	Alright … let me see. How about this one here?
1	*Shop assistant:*	Hello, can I help you?
☐	*Shop assistant:*	You're welcome. Goodbye!
☐	*Shop assistant:*	Okay … do you like this one here?
☐	*Shop assistant:*	That's 19,95.
☐	*Shop assistant:*	Okay … do you like that one over there?
☐	*Shop assistant:*	Okay … what colour?
☐	*Customer:*	Fine … thank you very much.
☐	*Customer:*	Yes, I do. But it is too expensive.
☐	*Customer:*	Hello. Yes, please. I want a new pullover.
☐	*Customer:*	No, I think it's too big.
14	*Customer:*	Goodbye!
☐	*Customer:*	Uhm … I like blue and green.
☐	*Customer:*	Yeah, it's nice. How much is it?

A day in the life of Valery

74 * * *

Listen to Valery talking about a day in her life and answer the questions.

	True	False
1 Valery gets up at half past six.	☐	☐
2 She has breakfast at seven.	☐	☐
3 Valery goes to work at quarter past eight.	☐	☐

4 Valery's school starts at ______________________.

5 Her school ends at ______________________.

6 She has dinner at ______________________.

7 From seven to eight Valery …
A watches TV B talks on the phone C often takes a bath

8 At half past nine she …
A goes to bed B goes to sleep C goes home

9 Until ten o'clock Valery …
A plays computer games B reads a book C listens to music

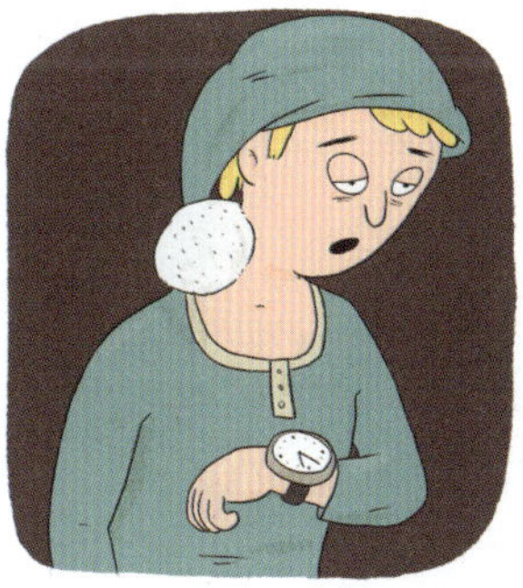

What are different people doing right now?

75 ✱✱✱

Listen to what different people are doing at the moment and put the sentences into the correct order *(Reihenfolge)*, the beginning and ending are given *(vorgegeben)*.

☐	Gaby is baking a cake for her family.
☐	Helen is looking for her cat.
☐	Kate is riding her horse in the park.
☐	Eric is writing a love poem.
12	Gabriel is ice-skating with his friends.
☐	Manuel is listening to loud music in his room.
☐	Ann is doing her homework.
1	Frank is talking on his phone.
☐	Christina is reading the newspaper.
☐	Peter is watching a long film on TV.
☐	Bill is playing a game with his brother.
☐	Irene is eating a banana.

E Hörübungen für die vierte Schularbeit

Party invitation

76 *

Listen to Melinda and Bethany talking about a party invitation *(Einladung)* and tick true or false.

	True	False
1 Melinda is going to have a party.	☐	☐
2 Her party is going to be on the weekend.	☐	☐
3 Bethany is not going to come to Melinda's party.	☐	☐
4 They are going to eat pizza and play games.	☐	☐
5 Bethany is going to bake a cake.	☐	☐
6 They are going to have a garden party at Melinda's house.	☐	☐
7 Melinda is going to invite six friends to her party.	☐	☐

Last weekend

77 * * *

Listen to Betty talking about her last weekend and answer the questions.

	True	False
1 Last weekend wasn't great for Betty.	☐	☐
2 Betty was at the cinema with a friend.	☐	☐
3 The film wasn't good.	☐	☐
4 Then they were at a pizza restaurant for dinner.	☐	☐

5 The pizzas ***were / weren't*** big and okay.

6 The friends ***were / weren't*** at a disco.

7 In the evening Betty ***was / wasn't*** tired.

8 After breakfast Betty ***was / wasn't*** at her friend's house.

9 For lunch the girls were at a sandwich place and the food ________________.

10 In the afternoon they were at a shopping centre for ________________.

11 In the evening Betty was back ________________.

12 For Betty the weekend was ________________.

Young love

78 ✱✱✱

Listen to a story about young love *(junge Liebe)* and answer the questions.

		True	False
1	When she was a young girl, she met a boy.	☐	☐
2	It was a nice day and she was at a party.	☐	☐
3	She sat under a tree and wrote a book.	☐	☐

4 She saw a cute *(süß)* boy. He ______________________________.

5 The boy looked at her and ______________________________.

6 Then he said: 'Hi, ______________________________.'

7 So the young girl said: …
A Hi, I'm Denise **B** Hi, I'm Doris **C** Hi, I'm Doreen

8 But his dog ran away and Toby …
A ran away too **B** came close to her **C** called his name

9 When he left the young girl heard him say …
A I'm sorry **B** I'm late **C** I'm hungry

Üben

DURCH STARTEN

ENGLISCH

HÖRVERSTÄNDNIS ÜBEN

Lösungen

1

VERITAS

Gemeinsam besser lernen

Lösungen und Niederschriften (*Transcripts*) aller Hörtexte

Die **Lösungen** und die **Lösungshinweise** in den Transcripts sind **blau** gedruckt.

Alphabet

1 Listen and underline the letters of the alphabet you hear.

A B C **D** E F **G** H **I** J **K** **L** M N **O** P Q **R** S T **U** V **W** X Y **Z**

Supergirl Lea

2 Listen to Lea introducing herself *(sich vorstellen)* and choose *am* / *is* / *are*.

Hi, my name **is** Lea.
I **am** from Austria.
I **am** ten years old.
I **am** at school in Gmunden.
I **am** in class 1A.
My telephone number **is** 0555 – 4213769.
My email address **is** lea.supergirl@yeah.com
I **am** a super girl!

June's email

3 Listen to a dialogue about June's email address and fill in the missing words.

Lena: Hi, I'm Lena. What's your **name**?
June: **Hi**, I'm June.
Lena: Hi, June. What's your **email / e-mail** address?
June: It's juneeliza@thatisme.com
Lena: **Can** you spell it for me?
June: Okay … j-u-n-e-e-l-i-z-a-at-t-h-a-t-i-s-m-e-dot-com.
Lena: **Thank** you, June.
June: Goodbye, Lena.
Lena: **Goodbye**!

Numbers

4 Listen and write down the numbers.

one
three
five
eight
twelve
fifteen
nineteen
twenty-two
twenty-four

Numbers and animals

5 Listen and fill in the numbers.

1 **two** insects
2 **three** gorillas
3 **twenty-one** bears
4 **four** crocodiles
5 **thirteen** frogs
6 **five** fish
7 **nineteen** rabbits
8 **twenty-five** cows

Frog meets bear

6 Listen to the dialogue and fill in the missing *(fehlende)* words.

Frog: Hi. **How** are you?
Bear: I'm **fine**, thanks. How are you?
Frog: I'm okay. What's your **name**?
Bear: My name is Jake. I'm a brown **bear**. And you?
Frog: I'm a green **frog**. I'm Jenny. I eat flies.
Bear: Well, **nice** to meet you, Jenny. Bye!
Frog: **Bye**, Jake!

Boy meets girl

7 Listen to the dialogue and fill in the missing words.

Girl: Hi, Daniel. How are **you**?
Boy: Hi, Susie. I'm fine. **How** are you?
Girl: I'm great. **Thanks**. I have to go now. Goodbye!
Boy: **Goodbye**, Susie!

Children meet

8 Listen to the children and fill in the missing words.

Boy: Hi, Julie. How **are you**?
Girl 1: I'm fine, **thank** you. How are you, Samuel?
Boy: I'm fine. Julie, **this is** Melanie.
Girl 1: **Hi**, Melanie.
Girl 2: Hi, Julie.
Girl 1: Nice to **meet you**.
Girl 2: Nice to meet you **too**.
Girl 1: Goodbye!
Girl 2: **Bye**!
Boy: Goodbye, Julie!

Strange plural forms

9 Listen and fill in the missing numbers and irregular *(unregelmäßige)* plural forms.

1 five **babies**
2 **ten babies**
3 seven **children**
4 **eleven children**
5 ten **boys**
6 **twenty boys**
7 fifteen **fish**
8 **two fish**

Alex

10 Listen to Alex introducing himself *(sich vorstellen)* and fill in the missing words.

1 Hi, **I'm** Alex.
2 I'm **ten** years old.
3 **I'm** from Austria.
4 I'm in class **1A**.
5 My email address **is** alexisgreat@hello.com.

Jim's schoolbag

11 Listen and underline the things in Jim's schoolbag.

pen
pencil
pencil case
pencil sharpener
paintbrush
ruler
rubber
glue stick
scissors
water colours

Transcript mit Lösungshinweisen:

Hello, I'm Jim. In my schoolbag there is a **pencil case** with a **pen** and a **ruler**. I have **scissors** and a **glue stick** in my school bag, too. Today I also have a **paintbrush** and **water colours** in my schoolbag. What is in your schoolbag?

Colours of classroom things

12 Listen and underline the correct colours of the classroom things.

1 glue stick – **blue**
2 exercise book – **orange**
3 pencil case – **pink**
4 paintbrush – **red**
5 pencil sharpener – **white**
6 ruler – **brown**
7 scissors – **grey**

Transcript mit Lösungshinweisen:

In our classroom there are many colourful things. The glue stick is **blue** and the exercise book is **orange**. The pencil case is **pink** and the paintbrush is **red**. The pencil sharpener is **white** and the ruler is **brown**. Oh, yeah, and the scissors are **grey**. Are the things in your classroom **colourful**?

School things

13 Listen to Greg and Gina talking about their school things and fill in the correct colours.

1 Gina's new school bag is **orange and blue**.
2 Greg's schoolbag is **green and black**.
3 Greg's pencil case is **brown and yellow**.
4 Gina's pencil case is **red**.
5 Gina's scissors are **red**.
6 Gina's pencil sharpener is **red**.
7 Greg's pencil sharpener is **black**.
8 Greg's scissors are **grey**.
9 Greg's ruler is **green**.
10 Greg's pen is **green**.
11 Gina's ruler is **brown**.
12 Gina's pen is **pink**.

Transcript mit Lösungshinweisen:

Greg: Hello Gina!
Gina: Hi Greg!
Greg: Wow! You have a nice **orange and blue schoolbag**. Is it new?
Gina: Yes it is, thanks. I like your **green and black school bag**. Is your pencil case also green and black?
Greg: No, **my pencil case is brown and yellow**. What colour is your pencil case?
Gina: My **pencil case is red**. I like red. I also have **red scissors and a red pencil sharpener**.
Greg: Oh, okay. My **pencil sharpener is black** and my **scissors are grey**. I like green. I have a **green ruler** and a **green pen**.
Gina: That is ni**ce! My ruler i**s brown **and my pen** is *pink*.
Greg: Ah, very colourful!

Colours in the classroom

14 Listen to Noah talking about the different colours of the things in his classroom and tick true or false.

1 The door is blue. **F**
2 The windows are white. **T**
3 The board is green. **F**
4 The desks are black. **F**
5 The computer is grey. **T**
6 The chairs are blue. **T**
7 The floor is orange. **F**
8 The CD player is pink. **F**
9 The classroom is colourful. **T**

Transcript mit Lösungshinweisen:

Hi, I'm Noah. There are many different colours in my classroom. The **door is green** and the **windows are white**. The **board is black** and the **desks are brown**. The **computer is grey** and the **chairs are blue**. The **floor is yellow** and the **CD player is red**. I like **my colourful classroom**.

Classroom imperatives

15 Listen to the teacher and write down the numbers in the correct order *(Reihenfolge)* of the imperatives *(Befehlsformen)*.

4 Take out your books!
3 Close the door!
6 Don't speak!
7 Clean the board!
1 Stand up!
8 Don't open the window!
5 Open your books!
2 Sit down!

Transcript mit Lösungshinweisen:

Hello! **Stand up**, please! Thank you! Good morning! Now **sit down**! Paula, please **close the door**! Thanks! Now **take out your books**! Okay, **open your books** on page ten! **Don't talk**, Martin! James, please **clean the board**! No Susie, **don't open the window**!

Teacher's commands

16 Listen to what the teacher tells the students to do and complete *(vervollständige)* the commands *(Befehle)*.

1 **Don't open** your books!
2 **Sit** down!
3 **Don't** talk!
4 **Stand** up!
5 **Clean** the board!
6 **Don't open** the window!
7 **Take out** your books!
8 **Close** the door!
9 **Open** the window!
10 **Don't stand** up!
11 **Don't sit** down!

In a terrarium

17 Listen to a dialogue of children looking into a terrarium and answer the questions about where the animals are.

1 Where is the snake? **The snake is under the rock.**
2 Where is the crab? **The crab is on the big rock.**
3 Where are the spiders? **The spiders are next to the leaf *(Blatt)*.**
4 What are the spiders behind? **The spiders are behind glass.**
5 Where are the spiders NOT? **The spiders are not on Tina.**

Transcript mit Lösungshinweisen:

Tina: Hey, there is a snake over there!
Tammy: Really, where?
Tina: **The snake is under the rock.**
Tammy: Yeah, now I see it! There it is. Do you see the crab in there, too?
Tina: What? No, I don't see a crab.
Tammy: Look … **the crab is on the big rock** over there.
Tina: Ah … you are right.
Tammy: And **the spiders are next to the leaf**.
Tina: Oh no, I hate spiders.
Tammy: **They are behind glass**. Don't worry! **The spiders are not on you**.
Tina: Yes, you are right. I don't want them on me! *(Ich will nicht, dass sie auf mir sind!)*

Tigers

18 Listen to Sara and Claire talking about tigers at the zoo and answer the questions.

1	The tiger is next to the bush.	**F**	(behind the bush)
2	The tiger is not very beautiful.	**F**	(it is beautiful)
3	Sara likes tigers.	**T**	
4	Claire likes tigers.	**F**	(doesn't really like tigers)
5	Tigers are big.	**T**	

Transcript mit Lösungshinweisen:

Claire: Wow, look at the tiger over there!
Sara: What tiger?
Claire: Sara look … **the tiger is behind the bush**.
Sara: Oh yeah … there it is!
Claire: Do you see it?
Sara: Yes, now I see the tiger. **It is beautiful**.
Claire: Do you like tigers?
Sara: Oh yes! … **I love tigers**!
Claire: Really?
Sara: Yes I do. Do you like tigers?
Claire: **I don't really like them**.
Sara: No?
Claire: No, **they are so BIG**!

Miguel's little sister, Lilly

19 Listen to Miguel talking about his sister and choose *am*/*is*/*are*.

Hi, I **am** Miguel.
I **am** six years old.
I have a sister.
She **is** Lilly.
She **is** four years old.
She **is** nice to me.
I **am** nice to her.
We **are** a family.

Julie's family

20 Listen to Julie talking about her family and fill in *am/is/are*.

1 Hi, my name **is** Julie.
2 I **am** 35 years old.
3 I **am** from America.
4 Daniel **is** my husband *(Ehemann)*.
5 He **is** also my best friend.
6 We **are** married *(verheiratet)*.
7 We **are** also parents.
8 Samuel and Melanie **are** our children.
9 Samuel **is** our son.
10 He **is** six years old.
11 Melanie **is** our daughter.
12 She **is** three years old.
13 We **are** a family.

David's desk

21 Listen to a description *(Beschreibung)* of David's desk and put the sentences into the correct order *(Reihenfolge)*.

7 I love my cool desk!
4 My grey CD-player is behind the pencil case.
2 On my desk there is a black laptop with a blue pencil case next to it.
5 In front of my pencil case there is my yellow exercise book.
3 In the pencil case there are green pencils and a pencil sharpener.
1 I have a wonderful new desk and all my school things are on it.
6 My orange ruler is under the exercise book.

Transcript:

I have a wonderful new desk and all my school things are on it.
On my desk there is a black laptop with a blue pencil case next to it.
In the pencil case there are green pencils and a pencil sharpener.
My grey CD-player is behind the pencil case.
In front of my pencil case there is my yellow exercise book.
My orange ruler is under the exercise book.
I love my cool desk!

Pirate Paula

22 Listen to Pirate Paula introducing herself *(sich vorstellen)* and tick *(kreuze an)* true or false.

1	Paula is a pirate.	T	
2	She has got a pelican on her shoulder.	F	(parrot)
3	She has got a dog next to her.	T	
4	Paula has got a wooden leg.	F	(no wooden leg)
5	Paula has not got a sword.	F	(has a sword)
6	The pirate has got pink hair.	F	(purple)
7	Paula, the pirate, hasn't got a big ship.	T	
8	She hasn't got a fast ship.	F	(has fast ship)
9	The pirate has got a tattoo on her arm.	T	
10	Paula has got purple shoes.	F	(no shoes on)

Transcript mit Lösungshinweisen:

Hello, my name is Paula and **I am a pirate**. I have got a **parrot on my left shoulder** and a **dog next to my right leg**. **I haven't got a wooden leg**. I **have got a long sword** which I like very much. **I have got purple hair** and a nose ring. **I haven't got a big ship**. My ship is small **and very fast**. I have got a big **tattoo on my arm**. **I haven't got shoes** on my feet.

Pirate Kate

23 Listen to Pirate Kate introducing herself *(sich vorstellen)* and tick *(kreuze an)* true or false.

1	Captain Kate has got blond hair and blue eyes.	F	(brown hair)
2	Pirate Kate has got a tattoo of a parrot on her arm.	F	(pelican)
3	Kate has not got a wooden leg.	T	
4	She has got a black and white dog.	F	(cat)
5	Pirate Kate has got a big nose with a ring in it.	F	(small nose)
6	She is very strong!	T	
7	Her father 'James the Joker' is also a pirate.	F	(brother)
8	James is not very funny.	F	(very funny)
9	He has got a small nose and red hair.	F	(big nose)
10	James has got a hook and a wooden leg.	T	
11	Pirate James has got a parrot.	T	

Transcript mit Lösungshinweisen:

Hello, my name is Captain Kate and I am a pirate. I have got **brown** hair and blue eyes. I have got a tattoo of a **pelican** on my right arm. I **haven't got a wooden leg**. I have got a black and white **cat**, I haven't got a dog. I have got a **small nose** with a ring in it. I am **very strong**! I have got a **brother** who is a pirate. His name is 'James the Joker'. He **is very funny**. He has got **a big nose** and red hair. He has got a **hook** on his left arm and a **wooden leg**. He hasn't got a dog or a cat, James the Joker **has got a parrot** that likes him very much. The parrot likes to laugh!

Feelings in the classroom

24 Listen to Tom describing the feelings of the children in the classroom and fill in the correct feelings.

1 Tom is **happy**.
2 Lisa is **excited**.
3 Ben is **angry**.
4 Lea is **nervous**.
5 Aaron is **hungry**.
6 Debbie is **cold**.
7 Vicky is **hot**.
8 Tina is **scared**.
9 Tom is **proud**.
10 Ann is **bored**.

Transcript mit Lösungshinweisen:

Hello Ann, I'm Tom. **I'm happy** to meet you.
This is Lisa. **She is also very excited** to meet you.
Oh, see? **Ben is angry**. He is not okay today.
And **Lea is nervous**. She is always nervous.
Ah, and that is **Aaron**, he **is hungry**. He likes chocolate!
Debbie is next to the window. She **is cold** so close the window, please!
It's not warm in here. That is **Vicky**, she **is hot** today.
Oh yeah, and **Tina** is behind the door. She **is scared**.
So … **I am proud** to show you my class.
Well **Ann**, how are you? Are you okay? Oh no, you are very **bored**.

Supermodel Jane

25 Listen to the description *(Beschreibung)* of a day in the life of Supermodel Jane and underline *(unterstreiche)* the correct feelings.

Jane is a supermodel. This is a day in the life of Jane the supermodel.
It is early in the morning and Jane is **tired**. She has got a beautiful body and a great job. Jane is **proud**.
At work there are many photographers. They have got cameras. They are excited. Jane is happy. She has a good job. She is not **nervous**.
At lunchtime Jane is **hungry**. She has not got a hamburger, she has got an apple. So Jane is **angry**.
In the afternoon it is **hot**. So Jane is very hot, she is not **cold**.
In the evening Jane is not at work. She is at home. She is **bored**. At night Jane is in bed. She is **tired**.

Barbara's week

26 Listen to Barbara talking about her week and connect *(verbinde)* the sentences.

On Monday **I am sad, I am not okay.**
On Tuesday **I am nervous, I have a test. I am not proud.**
On Wednesday **I am angry, I am not happy.**
On Thursday **I am cold, very cold. I am not hot.**
On Friday **I am happy, I have dance class. I love dancing.**
On Saturday **I am excited, it is the weekend! I am not bored!**
On Sunday **I am hungry. Oh! I am very hungry!**

Our band

27 Listen to the band leader *(Leiter)* Miguel introducing *(vorstellen)* himself and his band and fill in the missing words.

1 Miguel is the **singer**.
2 Melissa is the **drummer**.
3 Martin is the **bass guitar player**.
4 Marvin is the **keyboard player**.
5 Marcus is the **guitarist**.
6 Marie is the **saxophone player**.
7 M's is the **band name**.

Transcript mit Lösungshinweisen:

Hi, I'm Miguel and this is our band. Welcome! **I am the singer**. We are called the M's. This is why:
Melissa is our drummer. When she plays the drums it is loud!
Martin is our bass guitar player. He is very good, his fingers are so fast on his bass guitar!
Marvin is our keyboard player. He is a wonderful pianist!
Marcus is our guitarist. He is great on the guitar!
His sister **Marie is our saxophone player**. I like her a lot!
So all our names start with M and that is why **our band name is the M's**.

Samuel's family

28 Listen to Samuel talking about his family and fill in *I, you, he, she, it, we* or *they*.

Hi, I am Samuel.
I am six years old.
I have a big house and my own room.
I like **it**.
My daddy is 36 years old. **He** works in Vienna.
My mum is also 36 years old. **She** is a teacher.

Interview with Samuel

29 Listen to an interview with Samuel and choose the correct form of *I, you, he, she* or *it*.

Girl: Hello, what's your name?
Boy: Hello, my name is Samuel.
Girl: How old are **you**?
Boy: **I** am six years old.
Girl: Where do you live?
Boy: **I** live in Austria.
Girl: What is your house like?
Boy: **It** is big.
Girl: Okay … do **you** have a brother or a sister?
Boy: I have a sister.
Girl: What's her name?
Boy: Her name is Melanie.
Girl: How old is she?
Boy: **She** is four years old.
Girl: And what does your father do?
Boy: My father works in Vienna.
Girl: How old is **he**?
Boy: **He** is 36 years old.
Girl: And what does your mother do?
Boy: My mother goes to school.
Girl: Okay … and how old is **she**?
Boy: **She** is 36 years old.
Girl: And what is her job at school?
Boy: **She** is a teacher.
Girl: Okay, thank you very much. Have a good day. Goodbye!
Boy: Goodbye, Julie!

What Beth and Maria can and can't do

30 Listen to Beth and Maria talking about what they can and can't do and fill in the missing words.

Beth: Hi Maria!
Maria: Hi Beth!
Beth: Maria, look what I **can** do!
Maria: Wow Beth! You **can** wiggle your ears! That's great! I **can't** do that. What else **can** you do?
Beth: Well, I **can** stand on my hands. Do you want to see? I **can** show you.
Maria: Yes, please … Wow, you **can** really stand on your hands. I **can't** stand on my hands.
Beth: That's okay. What **can** you do?
Maria: Well, I **can** touch my nose with my tongue.

Beth: Really? **Can** you show me?
Maria: Yes, I **can** … see?
Beth: Oh, that is great! I **can't** touch my nose with my tongue.
Maria: Fine, but you **can** try.
Beth: Okay … hm … yeah! I **can** touch my nose with my tongue!
Maria: Oh, yes you **can** do it!

Mike's school day

31 Listen to Mike talking about his school day and fill in the missing words in present simple *(einfache Gegenwart)*.

1 In the morning I **get up** at seven and get ready.
2 Then I **go** to school. It is near my house.
3 There I **see** my friends. They are great!
4 We often laugh and **have** fun.
5 In English we **talk** to our partners. It is fun!
6 In music we **listen** to CDs. That is very loud!
7 In German we **write** a text about our families. It is so long!
8 Next we **eat** lunch. I love pizza! It is so good!
9 In gym we **run** very much. I am so tired!
10 That **is** my school day!

Milo, the cat

32 Listen to Patricia talking about her cat and answer the questions.

1	The cat Milo is four years old.	**T**	
2	Milo likes to drink water.	**F**	(milk)
3	The cat looks for dogs when she is outside.	**F**	(mice)

4 Milo loves to **sit on the couch**.
5 The cat is **small but fast**.
6 When Patricia comes home Milo **makes a lot of noise**.

7 Patricia carries **Milo around (sometimes).**
8 Milo sleeps **in her (little cat) bed.**
9 Milo is **a good cat / Patricia's best friend**.

Transcript mit Lösungshinweisen:

Hi, I'm Patricia and this is my cat Milo. She is **four** years old. I think Milo is my best friend. She likes to eat fish and **drink milk**. She eats my cookies too. **She looks for mice** when she is outside. Milo loves to **sit on the couch** by the window. There she watches the children play in the garden. Milo often plays with balls and toys. She is a very **small cat but she can run very fast**. When I come home from school Milo hears me and **makes a lot of noise**. I sometimes **carry Milo around**. She likes that. Milo goes to **sleep in her little cat bed** at night. She is **a good cat** and I love her very much.

What my family eats

33 Listen to a mother talking about what her family eats and answer the questions.

Elizabeth's family likes to eat noodles.	**T**	
They often eat rice.	**F**	(meat)
Elizabeth eats lots of salad.	**T**	
The children like vegetables.	**T**	
Daniel always eats cheese.	**F**	(never)
He doesn't like fish.	**T**	
The family usually has noodles with sausages.	**F**	(with meat and vegetables)
The children always have an apple with their breakfast.	**F**	(with lunch)
They sometimes have ice-cream as a snack.	**F**	(grapes)
The family often has pizza.	**T**	

Transcript mit Lösungshinweisen:

Hi, my name is Elizabeth and I want to talk about what my family likes to eat. We **often eat noodles** and **meat**. I like to eat **lots of salad** and vegetables. My **children like vegetables** but they do not eat salad. My husband Daniel always eats meat but **he never eats cheese**. He **doesn't like** cheese or **fish**. **We usually have noodles with meat and vegetables**. We sometimes have curry. My children always have a banana with their breakfast and an **apple with their lunch**. They often eat fruit. They usually have **grapes as a snack**. We **often have pizza** because we all love pizza so much!

Dialogue about clothes

34 Listen to Mia and Marcy talking about clothes and choose the correct words.

Mia: Hi Marcy!
Marcy: Hey Mia!
Mia: Wow, Marcy I love your **sweater** … is it new?
Marcy: Yes, thanks … it is. I **don't often** wear pink but I like this new pink sweater.
Mia: **Do** you buy your own clothes?
Marcy: Yes, I do … And you? Do you buy your own **clothes** too?
Mia: No, I **don't**.
Marcy: So, **does** your mum buy your clothes for you?
Mia: Yes, she does. She knows that I like to wear dresses and **skirts**. I have a new dress!
Marcy: That's nice. What colour is your new **dress**?
Mia: Uhm … **it's** blue and yellow and white.
Marcy: Well that **dress** sounds nice!
Mia: Do you like to wear **dresses**?
Marcy: No, I don't like to wear dresses or skirts. I often wear jeans and **T-shirts**.

Lilly's dream pet

35 Listen to an interview about Lilly's dream pet and answer the questions.

Lilly: Hello!
Alara: Hi, tell me about your dream pet.
Lilly: Well, my dream pet is a unicorn!
Alara: **What**?
Lilly: A unicorn ... that is my favourite pet.
Alara: Okay ... **what's its name**?
Lilly: It's Mr. Perfect.
Alara: I understand ... **where does Mr. Perfect live**?
Lilly: Mr. Perfect lives in a stable in my garden. He has a lot of room.
Alara: Alright ... **what does he eat**?
Lilly: He eats lots of hay *(Heu)*, just like a horse, and also fruit.
Alara: Sure ... **how often do you feed him**?
Lilly: I feed my favourite pet five times a day.
Alara: Wow! That's really a lot!
Lilly: Yes, my unicorn is BIG!
Alara: One last question: **Is your unicorn real**?
Lilly: No! My unicorn is a dream pet!

Problems with unusual pets

36 Listen to Taylor's problems with his unusual pet and fill in the missing object pronouns *me, you, him, her, it, us* or *them*.

Let me tell you about a problem I have with my unusual pet. It is a crocodile and I love **him**!
I call him Mr. Long because he has a lot of very long teeth. The problem is that I have to clean **them**!
It takes me a very long time to do it and I don't like to brush Mr. Long's teeth. Can you understand **me**?
I really like my unusual pet and I know that Mr. Long likes **me**.
We can play in the swimming pool and he is nice to **me**.
I just have another problem: I can't pet **him**.
It hurts because he is not very soft and comfortable. He's a crocodile and I can feel **it**.
One more problem is that Mr. Long likes to play outside. There he looks for bugs *(Käfer)* and mice and when he finds some, Mr. Long brings them to **us**.
It is strange because I don't like bugs and mice. I hate **them**!

Shopping dialogue

37 Listen to a shopping dialogue and put the sentences into the correct order *(Reihenfolge)*, the beginning and ending are given *(vorgegeben)*.

15 *Shop assistant:* That's 9,95.
7 *Shop assistant:* Do you like that one over there?
13 *Shop assistant:* Would you like this one here?
1 *Shop assistant:* Hello, can I help you?
3 *Shop assistant:* What colour?
5 *Shop assistant:* Let me see. How about this one here?
17 *Shop assistant:* You're welcome. Goodbye!
9 *Shop assistant:* Would you like one of those caps over there?
11 *Shop assistant:* Then what cap would you like?

14 *Child:* How much is it?
2 *Child:* Hello. Yes, please. I want a new cap.
16 *Child:* That's perfect. Thank you very much.
6 *Child:* No, I think it's too big.
12 *Child:* One of these right here, please.
10 *Child:* No, they do not look cool.
8 *Child:* Yes, I do. But it is too expensive.
18 *Child:* Goodbye!
4 *Child:* I like black and red.

Transcript mit Lösungshinweisen:

Shop assistant: Hello, can I help you?
Child: Hello. Yes, please. I want a new cap.
Shop assistant: Okay … **what colour**?
Child: Uhm … **I like black and red**.
Shop assistant: Alright … **let me see. How about this one here?**
Child: **No, I think it's too big.**
Shop assistant: Okay … **do you like that one over there?**
Child: **Yes, I do. But it is too expensive.**
Shop assistant: I understand … and **would you like one of those caps over there?**
Child: **No, They do not look cool.**
Shop assistant: Alright … **then what cap would you like?**
Child: **One of these right here, please.**
Shop assistant: Okay … **would you like this one here?**
Child: Yeah … **how much is it?**
Shop assistant: **That's 9,95.**
Child: **That's perfect. Thank you very much.**
Shop assistant: You're welcome. Goodbye!
Child: Goodbye!

How much is / are

38 Listen to the shopping dialogue and fill in how much *is/are*.

Shop assistant: Hello, can I help you?
Tom: Hi! Yes, please. **How much is** that sweater?
Shop assistant: That sweater is 19,50.
Tom: Okay, **how much are** those jeans?
Shop assistant: Those jeans are 25,90.
Tom: Alright, **how much is** this hat?
Shop assistant: This hat is 7,95.
Tom: And **how much are** these shoes?
Shop assistant: Those shoes are 15,90.
Tom: Fine, thank you.
Shop assistant: What would you like?
Tom: I don't want anything, thanks.

Midnight in Vienna

39 Listen to the time differences *(Zeitunterschiede)* and write down the correct times.

1 When it's midnight in Vienna what's the time in New York?
It's six p.m.

2 When it's midnight in Vienna what's the time in London?
It's eleven p.m.

3 When it's midnight in Vienna what's the time in Sydney?
It's ten a.m.

4 When it's midnight in Vienna what's the time in Tokyo?
It's eight a.m.

5 When it's midnight in Vienna what's the time in Moscow?
It's two a.m.

6 When it's midnight in Vienna what's the time in Cairo?
It's one a.m.

A day in the life of Vicky

40 Listen to Vicky talking about a day in her life and answer the questions.

1 Vicky gets up at half past six. **T**
2 She has breakfast at seven. **F** (a quarter to seven)
3 School starts at a quarter past eight. **F** (a quarter to eight)

4 Vicky goes to ballet class at **half past two.**
5 Vicky plays with her friends from **four to six.**
6 She has dinner with her family at **half past six.**

7 From seven to eight Vicky **watches TV.**
8 At half past eight she **goes to bed.**
9 Until nine o'clock Vicky **reads a book.**

Transcript mit Lösungshinweisen:

I **get up at half past six**. Then I get dressed and have **breakfast at a quarter to seven**. At seven o'clock I go to school. **School starts at a quarter to eight** and usually ends at a quarter past one. Then I go home and have lunch. Next I do my homework and go to **ballet class at half past two**. After ballet I meet my friends and **play with them from four to six**. At **half past six I have dinner** with my family. From **seven to eight I often watch TV**. At **half past eight I go to bed** and **read a book until nine o'clock**. That is a day in my life.

Phone conversation

41 Listen to a phone conversation *(Gespräch)* about what different people are doing at the moment and fill in present progressive.

1 Ben **is doing nothing (right now).**
2 Lea **is watching an interesting film (on TV).**
3 Jeff **is playing football (with his friends outside).**
4 Jane **is riding her horse (at the moment).**
5 Lea's dad **is working on the computer.**
6 Lea's mum **is cooking dinner / making spaghetti.**
7 Ben **is walking to Lea's / her house (at the moment).**

Transcript mit Lösungshinweisen:

Ben: Hi Lea, How are you?
Lea: Hi Ben, I'm fine, thanks. How are you?
Ben: Well, I'm bored. **I am doing nothing right now.** What are you doing?
Lea: I'm watching an interesting film on TV.
Ben: That sounds nice. What is your brother doing?
Lea: **Jeff is playing football with his friends outside.**
Ben: Oh, that sounds fun. And what is your sister doing?
Lea: **Jane is riding her horse at the moment.**
Ben: Wow, and what are your parents doing?
Lea: Uhm … **my dad is working on the computer and my mum is cooking dinner.**
Ben: Okay, what is she cooking?
Lea: I think **she is making spaghetti.**
Ben: That sounds really good.
Lea: Do you want to come over?
Ben: Yes, **I am walking to your house at the moment.**
Lea: Okay, see you soon!
Ben: Alright, Bye!
Lea: Bye, Ben!

What are different people doing right now?

42 Listen to what different people are doing at the moment and put the sentences into the correct order *(Reihenfolge)*, the beginning and ending are given *(vorgegeben)*.

3 Amy is doing her homework.
7 Barney is playing a game with his friend.
12 Christine is reading a book.
10 Danielle is texting her boyfriend on her phone.
14 Eliza is writing a long text.
1 Francis is swimming in our pool.
15 Greg is skateboarding with his classmates.
5 Hannah is looking after her three cats.
13 Iris is having a snack.
6 Jane is cooking dinner for her family.
8 Karin is riding her bike to school.
2 Lorenz is talking to his neighbour.
11 Mike is listening to music on the couch.
9 Nico is eating chocolate in bed.
4 Pete is watching a funny film in the living room.

Transcript:

Francis is swimming in our pool.
Lorenz is talking to his neighbour.
Amy is doing her homework.
Pete is watching a funny film in the living room.
Hannah is looking after her three cats.
Jane is cooking dinner for her family.
Barney is playing a game with his friend.
Karin is riding her bike to school.
Nico is eating chocolate in bed.
Danielle is texting her boyfriend on her phone.
Mike is listening to music on the couch.
Christine is reading a book.
Iris is having a snack.
Eliza is writing a long text.
Greg is skateboarding with his classmates.

Birthday invitation

43 Listen to Ann and Beth talking about a birthday invitation *(Einladung)* and tick true or false.

1	Ann is going to have a birthday party.	**T**	
2	Her birthday party is going to be on the seventh.	**F**	(next weekend)
3	Beth is not going to come to Ann's birthday party.	**F**	(she is going to come)
4	They are going to eat cake and play games.	**T**	
5	Ann's mum is not going to bake a cake.	**F**	(she is going to bake a cake)
6	They are going to have a garden party at Ann's house.	**T**	
7	Ann is going to invite seven friends to her party.	**F**	(six friends)
8	Beth is going to buy Ann a birthday present.	**T**	

Transcript mit Lösungshinweisen:

Ann: Hi Beth!
Beth: Hello Ann!
Ann: **I am going to have a birthday party** and I hope you can come.
Beth: Okay, sounds great. When is your birthday?
Ann: My birthday is on the seventh but **I am going to have my party on the tenth because it's the weekend.**
Beth: I understand. Yes, I can come to your birthday party on the tenth.
Ann: Wonderful! **We are going to eat cake and play games!** It's going to be fun!
Beth: Lovely! Is your mum going to bake a cake?
Ann: Yes, **she is and I am going to help her make a very big cake!**
Beth: Yummy! That sounds good. Are we going to be at your house?
Ann: Yes, **we are going to have a garden party**.
Beth: That's nice. And how many friends are you going to invite?
Ann: Hm … **I'm going to invite six friends** and I am happy that you can come to my party!
Beth: Great! Then **I'm going to buy you a wonderful present!**

Tina's and Tom's date

44 Listen to Tina and Tom talking about when they can go to the cinema and fill in the correct dates.

1 Tina has a tennis match on the **tenth**.
2 Tina has a friend's birthday party on the **eleventh**.
3 Tom has a football match on the **twelfth**.
4 Tom has a big family dinner party on the **thirteenth**.
5 Tina has a test on the **fifteenth**.
6 Tina has to study on the **fourteenth**.
7 Tom has a concert on the **fifteenth**.
8 Tina has a ski trip from the sixteenth to the **twenty-first**.
9 Tina and Tom can go to the cinema **today / right now**.

Transcript mit Lösungshinweisen:

Tina: Hi Tom!
Tom: Hi Tina! So, when do you have time to go to the cinema with me?
Tina: Well, let me see. **I have a tennis match on the tenth and a friend's birthday party on the eleventh.** What do you have on the twelfth?
Tom: Oh, I have a **football match on the twelfth** and **a big family dinner party on the thirteenth**. How about the fourteenth?
Tina: Uhm … I think I have a **test on the fifteenth** so I must **study on the fourteenth**.
Tom: Okay, I understand but I have a **concert on the fifteenth**. Can we go to the cinema on the sixteenth?
Tina: I'm sorry, no because then I am on a **ski trip until the twenty-first**. But we can go to the cinema on the twenty-second … What do you think?
Tom: The twenty-second? That's in two weeks! I say **we go to the cinema today**. What do you think about that?
Tina: Today is perfect … **We can go right now!**

Arielle's birthday plans

45 Listen to Arielle talking about her birthday plans and put the sentences into the correct order *(Reihenfolge)*.

2 I am going to have a party at my house.
11 At night we are going to talk and eat sweets.
8 I am going to get a lot of presents and play with them.
4 First we are going to play games in the house and also in the garden.
5 Then we are going to eat chips and drink Cola.
7 Later we are going to make a disco and dance to cool music.
1 My birthday is on the nineteenth and that is a Friday this year.
13 It's going to be the best birthday of my life!
6 My mum is going to make a pink birthday cake because that is my favourite colour.
9 Then my friends are all going to sleep at my house.
3 I am going to invite my three best friends and we are going to have lots of fun.
10 In the evening we are going to watch funny films and eat popcorn.
12 In the morning we are going to be tired and we are not going to get up early.

Transcript:

1 My birthday is on the nineteenth and that is a Friday this year.
2 I am going to have a party at my house.
3 I am going to invite my three best friends and we are going to have lots of fun.
4 First we are going to play games in the house and also in the garden.
5 Then we are going to eat chips and drink Cola.
6 My mum is going to make a pink birthday cake because that is my favourite colour.
7 Later we are going to make a disco and dance to cool music.
8 I am going to get a lot of presents and play with them.
9 Then my friends are all going to sleep at my house.
10 In the evening we are going to watch funny films and eat popcorn.
11 At night we are going to talk and eat sweets.
12 In the morning we are going to be tired and we are not going to get up early.
13 It's going to be the best birthday of my life!

Last night

46 Listen to John and Lisa talking about where they were last night and underline *(unterstreiche)* the correct forms.

John: Hi, Lisa.
Lisa: Hey, John.
John: Were you **at home** last night? I came to your house but your family was not there.
Lisa: Really? When were you at **my house** last night?
John: I was at your house at half past seven.
Lisa: At half past seven I was in **the bathtub** because I was **cold**. I was at home.
John: Were your parents at home?
Lisa: Yes, my parents were at home. They were in the **kitchen**. They were **hungry**.
John: Okay, was your brother at home?
Lisa: Uhm … oh my brother was in the **living room**. The TV was on. He was **scared**.
John: Was your sister at home?
Lisa: No, she was not at home. Sue was in the **park** with her boyfriend. She was **happy**. They were **alone**. When were you at home?
John: I was at my house at eight p.m. I was in my **bedroom**. I was angry.
Lisa: I am **sad** you were not with us.

Last weekend

47 Listen to Benny talking about his last weekend and answer the questions.

1	Last weekend wasn't great for Benny.	**F**	(was wonderful)
2	Benny was at the cinema with a friend.	**T**	
3	The film wasn't good.	**F**	(was good)
4	The boys were at a Chinese restaurant for dinner.	**F**	(burger restaurant)

5 The boys **were** at a bowling centre.
6 In the evening Benny **was** tired.
7 In the morning he **wasn't** tired.
8 After breakfast Benny **was** at his friend's house.

9 For lunch the boys were at a pizza place but the food **wasn't very good**.
10 In the afternoon they were at a shopping centre for **a (very) long time**.
11 In the evening Benny was **at home / on the couch / in front of the TV**.
12 For Benny the weekend was **very nice**.

Transcript mit Lösungshinweisen:

Last **weekend was wonderful**! I was at the **cinema with a friend**. The **film was great**! It was about super big spiders that ate … Well, you can watch the film yourself. Then **we were at a burger restaurant for dinner**. The burgers were big and very good. Afterwards **we were at a bowling centre**. It was fun. In the evening, when I was **at home I was very tired**. In the **morning I wasn't tired** and **after breakfast I was at my friend's house** to play computer games. It was really a lot of fun. For lunch we were at a pizza place but the **food wasn't very good**. In the afternoon we were at a shopping centre. We were there **for a very long time** … it wasn't cheap! In the evening, **I was back at home**. **I was on the couch in front of the TV**. It was really a **very nice weekend**.

Yesterday

48 Yesterday at seven o'clock Jonathan was on the phone with Susan. There was a lot going on at her house. Listen to her story and tick true or false.

1	Yesterday at seven o'clock the family wasn't busy.	**F**	(all busy)
2	Susan's brother was in his room at his desk.	**T**	
3	He wasn't angry.	**F**	(was angry)
4	Susan wasn't in the bathtub.	**F**	(in the bathtub)
5	Susan's sister was warm and relaxed.	**T**	
6	Susan was on the couch.	**T**	
7	She was bored.	**F**	(not bored)
8	Susan's dad was at home.	**F**	(at work)
9	He was not happy.	**T**	
10	He was angry.	**F**	(tired)
11	Susan's mum was in the kitchen.	**T**	
12	She was hungry.	**T**	
13	Yesterday at seven Jonathan wasn't at home.	**F**	(at home)

Transcript mit Lösungshinweisen:

Yesterday at seven o'clock there was a lot going on at my house. **We were all busy**.
My **brother was in his room**. He was **at his desk**. He was **angry**.
My **sister was in the bathtub**. It was **warm**. She was **relaxed**. She was not cold.
I was in the living room. **I was on the couch** in front of the TV. I **was not bored**.
My **dad was still at work**. He was **not at home**. He was **not happy**. He was **tired**.
My mum was in the kitchen. She was **hungry**.
So Jonathan, where were you yesterday at seven? Oh yeah … **you were at home** on the phone with me.

Ambulance / Fire Brigade / Police

49 Listen to the different phone conversations and fill in the missing information.

Dialogue 1

Rescue: Ambulance, fire brigade or police?
Child: **Ambulance**, please.
...
Ambulance: Hello, **how can I help you**?
Child: I need to go to the **hospital**! I jumped in the trampoline and now there is blood on my head.
Ambulance: What's the **address**?
Child: I live in **Beethoven Street** 23.
Ambulance: Can you **spell it for me**, please?
Child: Yes, It's **B-double E-T-H-O-V-E-N**.
Ambulance: **Okay, we are** on our way.

Dialogue 2

Rescue: Ambulance, fire brigade or **police**?
Child: Police, **please**.
...
Police: **Hello**, how can I help?
Child: There was a robbery **at the supermarket**!
Police: Okay, **what's the address**?
Child: I am in **Hoodwire Street 17**.
Police: **Can you spell it** for me, please?
Child: Yes, It's **H-double O-D-W-I-R-E.**
Police: **Thank you**, we are on our way.

Dialogue 3

Rescue: **Ambulance**, fire brigade or police?
Child: **Fire brigade**, please.
...
Fire Brigade: How can **I help**?
Child: **There is a fire** in my kitchen!
Fire Brigade: Oh, **what's the address**?
Child: I live in **Kaiserroll Street 5**.
Fire Brigade: Uhm ... Can you **spell it, please**?
Child: It's **K-A-I-S-E-double R-O-double L**.
Fire Brigade: Okay, we are **on our way**.

Lösungen

Rescue from a fire

50 Listen to a story about a fire and put the sentences into the correct order *(Reihenfolge)*.

8 There was a fire!
14 The family watched the fire brigade stop the fire.
7 When she arrived back in the kitchen she jumped!
3 The children were in the bathtub, they were warm.
10 She shouted 'Help!' and spelled the address of her house.
12 They rescued the children from the bathtub.
1 On Wednesday 17th there was a fire in a kitchen.
4 The children called their mum and she walked upstairs to the bathroom.
5 The children played in the water and they were happy.
15 In the end the family was happy and safe, but sad that the kitchen was broken.
13 The children were cold and scared.
6 Suddenly the mother smelled smoke.
9 She tried to stop it but the fire was too big, so she phoned the fire brigade.
2 The mother cooked dinner because the family was hungry.
11 Next she waited for five minutes and then the fire brigade arrived.

Transcript:

1 On Wednesday 17th there was a fire in a kitchen.
2 The mother cooked dinner because the family was hungry.
3 The children were in the bathtub, they were warm.
4 The children called their mum and she walked upstairs to the bathroom.
5 The children played in the water and they were happy.
6 Suddenly the mother smelled smoke.
7 When she arrived back in the kitchen she jumped!
8 There was a fire!
9 She tried to stop it but the fire was too big, so she phoned the fire brigade.
10 She shouted 'Help!' and spelled the address of her house.
11 Next she waited for five minutes and then the fire brigade arrived.
12 They rescued the children from the bathtub.
13 The children were cold and scared.
14 The family watched the fire brigade stop the fire.
15 In the end the family was happy and safe, but sad that the kitchen was broken.

Manuel's afternoon

51 Listen to Manuel talking about his afternoon and fill in the missing verbs in past simple *(Mitvergangenheitsform)*.

Yesterday **was** a very sunny day.
After school I **walked** home.
I was happy because my mother **cooked** lasagne for lunch.
Later I **phoned** my friend Niklas in the afternoon.
Next I **waited** for fifteen minutes and then Niklas **arrived**.
We **played** football outside and then it **happened**.
Niklas **stopped** and **pushed** me.
I was hurt and so I **shouted** at him.
He **helped** me up and **carried** me back inside the house.
After that I **wanted** to rest and so we **watched** TV on the couch.
Finally Niklas **waved** goodbye and **walked** back home.

TV habits

52 Listen to Claudia and Patrick talking about their TV habits *(Gewohnheiten)* and tick true or false.

Claudia:

Claudia usually watches TV for about three hours every day.	**F**	(two hours)
Claudia likes to watch cartoons when she eats breakfast.	**T**	
She watches science fiction shows before she goes to bed.	**F**	(quiz and reality shows)
Her parents usually watch the news at eight o'clock.	**T**	
Her brother sometimes watches sports programmes.	**F**	(nature programmes)

Patrick:

Patrick usually watches TV for about two hours on the weekend.	**F**	(four hours)
He sometimes watches sports programmes after lunch.	**T**	
On the weekend Patrick watches movies with his family.	**T**	
His little sister likes films about animals.	**F**	(princesses and ballerinas)
Patrick likes to watch films about superheroes.	**T**	

Transcript mit Lösungshinweisen:

Hi, I'm Claudia and I usually watch TV for about **two hours** every day. I **like to watch cartoons** in the morning when I eat breakfast and **quiz shows or reality shows** in the evening before I go to bed. My parents usually **watch the news** in the evening when I go to bed **around eight o'clock**. My brother sometimes watches **nature programmes** but I don't really like them.

Hi, I'm Patrick. I usually watch TV for about an hour every day and for **about four**

Bitte umblättern! ↺

hours on the weekend. I sometimes watch sports programmes after lunch to relax before I do my homework. On the weekend I like to watch movies on TV with my family. My little sister always wants to watch films about princesses and ballerinas but I think they are boring. I like to watch films about superheroes.

Past Tense

53 Listen and write down the irregular past tense forms.

1 did
2 froze
3 ran
4 bought
5 saw
6 said
7 sold
8 took
9 thought
10 was
11 went
12 had
13 read
14 paid
15 were
16 heard
17 sat
18 put
19 rang
20 held

Barbara's bad dream

54 Listen to Barbara talking about her bad dream and choose the correct past forms *(Mitverganganheit)*.

Last night I **read** a scary book and then I **went** to bed.
I **had** a bad dream and I **woke** up in the night.
I **thought** it was real and I **was** scared.
Next I **heard** a strange noise and **sat** up in bed.
Then I **saw** a light and **froze**.
Suddenly I **ran** into my parents' room and I **held** my mum's hand.

Young love

55 Listen to a story about young love and answer the questions.

1 When the man was young he met a girl. **T**
2 He saw her after school and phoned her. **F** (thought she was great)
3 They went to the park and sat on a bench. **F** (sat under a tree)

4 There they held hands and **thought about their future**.
5 They had a good time because **they were together**.
6 The young man put his arm around her and **read a love poem**.

7 They took a walk and **ran in the grass**.
8 But the young man froze because **the girl said: 'I love you!'**
9 When he heard her say it, suddenly **the man ran away**.

Transcript mit Lösungshinweisen:

When I was young **I met a girl**.
I saw her after school and **thought she was great**.
So we went to the park and **sat under a tree**.
There we held hands and **thought about the future**.
We had a good time because **we were together**.
I put my arm around her and **read a love poem**.
We took a walk and **ran in the grass**.
But I froze because **the girl said: 'I love you!'**
When I heard her say it, **I suddenly ran away**.

Princess Grace

56 Listen to a story about Princess Grace and fill in the missing words.

Hello, my **name** is Grace.
I want to tell you about my **life**.
When I was a little **girl** I watched a movie with a very beautiful actress.
That was when I decided that I also wanted to **be** an actress.
I went to **school** and studied very hard and after a while my dream came true.
I **was** an actress!
I played in many movies and I soon became a **star**.
One day I met a very **nice** young man and we got along very well.
We went out and we had a lot of fun and soon we fell in **love**.
He told **me** that he was a prince and I was so surprised and shocked!
I couldn't believe **it**!
Soon he asked me to be **his** wife and I said: 'YES!'
We **got** married.
I love my prince so **much** and now I am Princess Grace.
Somedays my life seems **like** a dream!

Arruba's story

57 Listen to Arruba's story and answer the questions.

1	Arruba is called the king of the desert.	**F**	(queen of the desert)
2	She thinks her name is interesting.	**T**	
3	She didn't travel a lot when she was young.	**F**	(father took her to many different countries)
4	Arruba's dad travelled for work.	**T**	
5	She liked eating desserts.	**F**	(loved the desert)
6	Arruba likes riding bikes.	**F**	(riding camels)
7	She likes the quiet desert.	**T**	
8	People asked Arruba questions about the desert.	**T**	
9	They wanted to learn about the desert.	**T**	
10	Arruba is not called the queen of the desert.	**F**	(she is called the queen of the desert)

Transcript mit Lösungshinweisen:

Hello, I want to tell you my story. I am called the **queen of the desert**. I know that sounds strange but this is how I got that **interesting name**.
When I was a little girl, I liked to travel, very much. My father took **me to many different countries**. He was a historian and **he travelled for his job**. He often took me with him and we went to different places. Soon I discovered that **I loved the desert**.
I love going to places that are hot. **I love riding on camels**. I love being surrounded by sand and nothing else. **I love that it's quiet** and that there is no stress and no noise around you.
One day I decided to study the desert and to become an expert on the desert. That was not hard because I spent so much time in the desert. **People came to ask me questions**. They **wanted to know more about the desert**. They wanted to hear what I learned in my many years in the hot desert. That is when **I got the name the queen of the desert**.

B Lösungen für die erste Schularbeit

Mia is great

58 Listen to Mia introducing herself *(sich vorstellen)* and choose *am/is/are*.

Hello, how **are** you?
My name **is** Mia.
I **am** from England.
I **am** 15 years old.
I **am** at school in London.
I **am** in class 5B.
My telephone number **is** 0678 – 9753246.
My email address **is** miaisgreat@home.com
I **am** a great girl!
And how **are** you?

Numbers

59 Listen to the numbers and write them down.

7
13
9
4
11
2
15
6
21

Mouse meets elephant

60 Listen to the dialogue and fill in the missing *(fehlende)* words.

Mouse: Hi. **How** are you?
Elephant: Hi, I'm **fine**. How are you?
Mouse: I'm okay. What's your **name**?
Elephant: My name is Eliot. I'm a grey elephant. And **you**?
Mouse: I'**m** a brown mouse. I'm Minnie. I eat cheese.
Elephant: **Nice** to meet you, Minnie. I eat mice!
Mouse: Oh no! **Bye**!

Dialogue

61 Listen to the dialogue and fill in the missing *(fehlende)* words.

Jules: Hi, Dee. **How** are you?
Dee: Hi, Jules. I'm fine, thanks. How **are** you?
Jules: **I'm** great. How is your brother?
Dee: He is okay, **thanks**. I have to go now.
Jules: Have a nice day! **Bye**!
Dee: Bye!

Strange plural forms

62 Listen and fill in the numbers and irregular *(unregelmäßige)* plural forms.

1 fifteen **boys**
2 **seven boys**
3 two **babies**
4 **nineteen babies**
5 three **fish**
6 **fourteen fish**
7 twenty-one **children**
8 **six children**

Colours of classroom things

63 Listen and underline the correct colours of the classroom things.

pencil case – **purple**
paintbrush – **black**
pencil sharpener – **white**
ruler – **blue**
glue stick – **grey**
exercise book – **yellow**
scissors – **green**
book – **brown**

Transcript mit Lösungshinweisen:

The things in my classroom are very colourful. The pencil case is **purple** and the paintbrush is **black**. The pencil sharpener is **white** and the ruler is **blue**. The glue stick is **grey** and the exercise book is **yellow**. The scissors are **green** and the book is **brown**.

Colours in the classroom

64 Listen to Norah talking about the different colours of the things in her classroom and tick true or false.

1	The door is blue.	**F**	(grey)
2	The windows are black.	**T**	
3	The board is green.	**T**	
4	The desks are black.	**F**	(brown)
5	The computer is white.	**T**	
6	The chairs are blue.	**F**	(orange)
7	The floor is orange.	**F**	(red)
8	The CD player is purple.	**T**	

Transcript mit Lösungshinweisen:

Hello, my name is Norah and there are many colours in my classroom. The **door is grey** and the **windows are black**. **The board is green** and the **desks are brown**. The **computer is white** and the **chairs are orange**. The **floor is red** and the **CD player is purple**. I like my colourful classroom!

Teacher's commands

65 Listen to what the teacher tells the students to do and complete *(vervollständige)* the commands *(Befehle)*.

1 **Stand** up!
2 **Close** the door!
3 **Sit** down!
4 **Take out** your books!
5 **Don't open** the window!
6 **Clean** the board!
7 **Don't** stand up!
8 **Don't** talk!

C Lösungen für die zweite Schularbeit

Giraffes

66 Listen to Sara and Claire talking about giraffes at the zoo and answer the questions.

1	The giraffe is next to the tree.	**F**	(behind the tree)
2	The giraffe is not beautiful.	**F**	(it is beautiful)
3	Sara likes giraffes.	**T**	
4	Claire likes giraffes.	**F**	(doesn't like them)
5	Giraffes are big.	**T**	

Transcript mit Lösungshinweisen:

Claire: Wow, look at the giraffe over there!
Sara: Where?
Claire: See … **the giraffe is behind the tree**.
Sara: Oh, there it is!
Claire: Can you see it?
Sara: Yes, I can see the giraffe. **It is so beautiful**!
Claire: Do you like giraffes?
Sara: Oh yes! **I love giraffes**!
Claire: Really?
Sara: Yes, I do. Do you like giraffes?
Claire: **I don't like them**.
Sara: What?
Claire: No, **they are so BIG**!

Deena's family

67 Listen to Deena talking about her family and fill in *am/is/are*.

1 Hi, my name **is** Deena.
2 I **am** 26 years old.
3 I **am** from England.
4 It **is** lovely there.
5 My brother's name **is** Henry.
6 He **is** my baby brother.
7 My sister's name **is** Nina.
8 She **is** my big sister.
9 We **are** a family.

Princess Pia

68 Listen to Princess Pia introducing herself *(sich vorstellen)* and tick *(kreuze an)* true or false.

1	Pia is a princess.	**T**	
2	She has got a pelican on her shoulder.	**F**	(parrot)
3	She has got a dog next to her.	**F**	(cat)
4	Pia hasn't got a tattoo.	**T**	
5	Pia has got a sword.	**T**	
6	The princess has got purple hair.	**F**	(pink)
7	Pia, the princess has got a nose stud.	**T**	
8	She hasn't got a big castle.	**F**	(has got a big castle)

Transcript mit Lösungshinweisen:

Hello, my name is Pia and **I am a princess**. I have got a **parrot on my right shoulder** and a **cat next to my left leg**. I **haven't got a tattoo**. I **have got a long sword** which I like very much. I **have got pink hair** and a nose stud. **I haven't got a big castle**. My castle is small and **very beautiful**.

Belinda's week

69 Listen to Belinda talking about her week and connect *(verbinde)* the sentences.

On Monday **I am tired, I am not okay.**
On Tuesday **I am sad, I have a test.**
On Wednesday **I am hot, I am not cold.**
On Thursday **I am hungry, very hungry. I am angry!**
On Friday **I am nervous, I have music class.**
On Saturday **I am happy, I love the weekend!**
On Sunday **I am excited. Oh! I am very excited!**

Denise's family

70 Listen to Denise talking about her family and fill in *I, you, he, she, it, we* or *they*.

Hi, my name is Denise. **I** am sixteen years old.
I have a big brother.
He is 18 years old.
He is a student at university.
And my sister is 20. **She** is a manager.
My parents are from India. **They** live in a nice house.
It is very big.
We are a happy family.
Do **you** have a big family?

Marvin, the dog

71 Listen to Penny talking about her dog and answer the questions.

1 The dog Marvin is four years old. **F** (five years old)
2 Marvin likes to watch TV. **T**
3 The dog looks for balls when it is outside. **F** (plays with the balls)

4 Marvin loves to **sit on the couch.**
5 The dog plays with **dolls and toys.**
6 Marvin is **a big dog.**

7 Marvin cannot **run fast.**
8 Marvin **is a good dog.**
9 Penny loves **Marvin very much.**

Transcript mit Lösungshinweisen:

Hi, I'm Penny and this is my dog Marvin. He is **five** years old. Marvin is my best friend. He **likes** to sleep and **watch TV**. He eats dog food. When he is outside, **he plays with the balls**. Marvin loves to **sit on the couch** in front of the TV. There he watches children's shows. Marvin often plays with **dolls and toys**. He is a **very big dog but he cannot run fast**. My pet is a **good dog** and I love him very much.

D Lösungen für die dritte Schularbeit

Dialogue about clothes

72 Listen to Rebecca and Angela talking about clothes and choose the correct words.

Rebecca: Hi Angela!
Angela: Hey Rebecca!
Rebecca: Wow, Angela I love your **shirt** … is it new?
Angela: Yes, thanks … it is. I **often** wear blue. I like this colour.
Rebecca: **Do** you often buy clothes?
Angela: Yes, I do … And you? Do you also like to buy **clothes**?
Rebecca: No, I **don't**.
Angela: Really?
Rebecca: My **sister** gives me her clothes.
Angela: That's nice. Is that skirt **new**?
Rebecca: Yes, it is.
Angela: Well it's **nice**!
Rebecca: Do you like to wear **skirts**?
Angela: No, I don't like to wear skirts. I often wear jeans and **T-shirts**.

Shopping dialogue

73 Listen to a shopping dialogue and put the sentences into the correct order *(Reihenfolge)*, the beginning and ending are given *(vorgegeben)*.

5 *Shop assistant:* Alright … let me see. How about this one here?
1 *Shop assistant:* Hello, can I help you?
13 *Shop assistant:* You're welcome. Goodbye!
9 *Shop assistant:* Okay … do you like this one here?
11 *Shop assistant:* That's 19,95.
7 *Shop assistant:* Okay … do you like that one over there?
3 *Shop assistant:* Okay … what colour?

12 *Customer:* Fine … thank you very much.
8 *Customer:* Yes, I do. But it is too expensive
2 *Customer:* Hello. Yes, please. I want a new pullover.
6 *Customer:* No, I think it's too big.
14 *Customer:* Goodbye!
4 *Customer:* Uhm … I like blue and green.
10 *Customer:* Yeah, it's nice. How much is it?

Transcript:

Shop assistant: Hello, can I help you?
Customer: Hello. Yes, please. I want a new pullover.
Shop assistant: Okay … what colour?
Customer: Uhm … I like blue and green.
Shop assistant: Alright … let me see. How about this one here?
Customer: No, I think it's too big.
Shop assistant: Okay … do you like that one over there?
Customer: Yes, I do. But it is too expensive.
Shop assistant: Okay … do you like this one here?
Customer: Yeah, it's nice. How much is it?
Shop assistant: That's 19,95.
Customer: Fine … thank you very much.
Shop assistant: You're welcome. Goodbye!
Customer: Goodbye!

A day in the life of Valery

74 Listen to Valery talking about a day in her life and answer the questions.

1	Valery gets up at half past six.	**F**	(a quarter to seven)
2	She has breakfast at seven.	**T**	
3	Valery goes to work at quarter past eight.	**F**	(a quarter past seven)

4 Valery's school starts at **a quarter to eight.**
5 Her school ends at **half past eleven.**
6 She has dinner at **half past six.**

7 From seven to eight Valery **often takes a bath.**
8 At half past nine she **goes to bed.**
9 Until ten o'clock Valery **reads a book.**

Transcript mit Lösungshinweisen:

I get up at a quarter to seven. Then I get dressed and have **breakfast at seven o'clock**. At **a quarter past seven I go to work**. I work at school and **my school starts at a quarter to eight** and **usually ends at half past eleven**. Then I go home and have lunch. Next I go to the park and play with my dog. At **half past six I have dinner**. From **seven to eight I often take a bath**. At **half past nine I go to bed** and **I read a book until ten o'clock**. That is a day in my life.

What are different people doing right now?

75 Listen to what different people are doing at the moment and put the sentences into the correct order *(Reihenfolge)*, the beginning and ending are given *(vorgegeben)*.

5 Gaby is baking a cake for her family.
4 Helen is looking for her cat.
7 Kate is riding her horse in the park.
11 Eric is writing a love poem.
12 Gabriel is ice-skating with his friends.
8 Manuel is listening to loud music in his room.
2 Ann is doing her homework.
1 Frank is talking on his phone.
9 Christina is reading the newspaper.
3 Peter is watching a long film on TV.
6 Bill is playing a game with his brother.
10 Irene is eating a banana.

Transcript:

Frank is talking on his phone.
Ann is doing her homework.
Peter is watching a long film on TV.
Helen is looking for her cat.
Gaby is baking a cake for her family.
Bill is playing a game with his brother.
Kate is riding her horse in the park.
Manuel is listening to loud music in his room.
Christina is reading the newspaper.
Irene is eating a banana.
Eric is writing a love poem.
Gabriel is ice-skating with his friends.

E Lösungen für die vierte Schularbeit

Party invitation

76 Listen to Melinda and Bethany talking about a party invitation *(Einladung)* and tick true or false.

1	Melinda is going to have a party.	T	
2	Her party is going to be on the weekend.	T	
3	Bethany is not going to come to Melinda's party.	F	(she is going to come)
4	They are going to eat pizza and play games.	T	
5	Bethany is going to bake a cake.	F	(she is going to bake cookies)
6	They are going to have a garden party at Melinda's house.	F	(not a garden party)
7	Melinda is going to invite six friends to her party.	F	(five friends)

Transcript mit Lösungshinweisen:

Melinda: Hi Bethany!
Bethany: Hello Melinda!
Melinda: **I am going to have a party** next weekend and I hope you can come.
Bethany: Okay, sounds great. When is the party?
Melinda: Well, **I am going to have the party on Saturday at five**.
Bethany: I see. **Yes, I can come** to your party on Saturday.
Melinda: Wonderful! **We are going to eat pizza and play games**! It's going to be fun!
Bethany: Lovely! I can bake some cookies!
Melinda: Yummy! That sounds great!
Bethany: And how many friends are you going to invite?
Melinda: **I'm going to invite five friends** and we are going to have so much fun!
Bethany: Great! Then I'm going to come to your party next weekend!

Last weekend

77 Listen to Betty talking about her last weekend and answer the questions.

1 Last weekend wasn't great for Betty. **F** (was wonderful)
2 Betty was at the cinema with a friend. **T**
3 The film wasn't good. **F** (was great)
4 Then they were at a pizza restaurant for dinner. **T**

5 The pizzas **were** big and okay.
6 The friends **were** at a disco.
7 In the evening Betty **was** tired.
8 After breakfast Betty **was** at her friend's house.

9 For lunch the girls were at a sandwich place and the food **was (very) good.**
10 In the afternoon they were at a shopping centre for **a (very) long time.**
11 In the evening Betty was back **at home / tired.**
12 For Betty the weekend was **very nice.**

Transcript mit Lösungshinweisen:

Last **weekend was wonderful**! I was at the **cinema with a friend**. The **film was great**! It was about superman and he helped … Well, you can watch the film yourself. Then **we were at a pizza restaurant for dinner. The pizzas were big and okay.** Afterwards **we were at a disco**. It was fun. The music was very loud! In the evening, when I was **at home I was very tired**. In the morning, **after breakfast I was at my friend's house** to dance together. It was really a lot of fun. For lunch we were at a sandwich place and the **food was very good**. In the afternoon we were at a shopping centre. We were there **for a very long time**! It was great! In the evening when **I was back at home, I was tired**. It was really a **very nice weekend**.

Young love

78 Listen to a story about young love *(junge Liebe)* and answer the questions.

1 When she was a young girl, she met a boy. **T**
2 It was a nice day and she was at a party. **F** (in the park)
3 She sat under a tree and wrote a book. **F** (read a book)

4 She saw a cute *(süß)* boy. He **walked his dog.**
5 The boy looked at her and **waved.**
6 Then he said: 'Hi, **I'm Toby.'**

7 So the young girl said: **Hi, I'm Doris.**
8 But his dog ran away and Toby **called his name.**
9 When he left the young girl heard him say **I'm sorry.**

Transcript mit Lösungshinweisen:

When I was young **I met a boy.**
It was a nice day and I was **in the park.**
There I sat under a tree and **read a book.**
Suddenly I saw a very cute boy. He **walked his dog.**
The boy looked at me and **waved.**
Then he said: **'Hi, I'm Toby.'**
So I said: **'Hi, I'm Doris.'**
But suddenly his dog ran away and Toby **called his name.**
When he left I heard him say: **'I'm sorry!'**

Liebe Eltern!

Dieses Lernhilfebuch umfasst **alle wichtigen Lerninhalte zum Hörverständnis in der 1. Klasse in Englisch**. Damit ist Durchstarten **die ideale Lernhilfe während des Schuljahres zum Thema Hören**. Egal, welches Hörübungsthema in der Schule gerade besprochen wird, Durchstarten bietet dazu **umfangreiche Hörbungen** in drei Schwierigkeitsgraden. Sie müssen sich nicht mehr überlegen, wo Sie passende Übungen für Ihr Kind herbekommen oder wie Sie das Thema Ihrem Kind noch einmal verständlich erklären können – Durchstarten erledigt das für Sie!

Damit entlastet Sie Durchstarten und verhilft Ihnen zu einem entspannten Familienleben ohne Schul- und Notenstress.

Wie das Üben mit dem Buch **funktioniert**, lesen Sie bitte auf der **inneren Umschlagseite 2** nach.

Wo Sie das jeweils passende **Übungsthema** finden, steht vorne im **Inhaltsverzeichnis**.

Unsere Leitlinien

- Diese Durchstarten-Lernhilfe wurde **von erfahrenen PädagogInnen / LehrerInnen entwickelt**.
- Wir orientieren uns an den aktuellen **Anforderungen des österreichischen Lehrplans**.
- Diese Lernhilfe kann **unabhängig vom jeweils verwendeten Schulbuch** eingesetzt werden.
- Bei der Produktentwicklung haben wir den Fokus auf die Anforderungen und **Wünsche von Ihnen und Ihrem Kind** gelegt.
- Digitale Inhalte und Funktionen werden nur dort eingesetzt, wo sie das **Lernen sinnvoll unterstützen**.

Immer am neuesten Stand

Auf www.durchstarten.at/aktuell informieren wir Sie gratis über inhaltliche Neuerungen / Ergänzungen zum Buch.

Wir wünschen Ihnen und Ihrem Kind ein erfolgreiches Schuljahr in der 1. Klasse!

Ihr Durchstartenteam